To Die For

A Die for Me Novella

AMY PLUM

Interior Design by Jasmine Aurora / jasmineaurora.co.uk

To Die For / Amy Plum—1st edition
ISBN print book: 978-2-9575891-2-8

Also by Amy Plum

The Die for Me Series
Die for Me
Until I Die
If I Should Die
Die for Her
Die Once More
Inside the World of Die for Me

After the End
Until the Beginning
(a duology)

Dreamfall
Neverwake
(a duology)

Chapter One

The first time I died, it was by bullets. Totally my fault.

I had instigated a gun battle, having ratted on my mom's abusive, drug-dealing boyfriend—Frankie—hoping it would get him out of our lives. Instead, it got him dead…along with me and my brother. I was thirteen at the time.

Remember that. It's important.

The second time I died, it was arrow through the forehead. Six months later. Again…totally my fault. I threw a knife at Violette—the undead evil overlord who had ensured my thirteen-year-old corpse animated as an immortal bad guy. (Stick with me. I promise to explain.) My knife-in-the-chest didn't kill her; it just pissed her off. So, she ordered her archer to shoot me.

Bull's eye.

The third time, I drowned. Pure stupidity.

Bran had taken me to Brittany to recover from death number two. After a year, I'd become bored—so I taught myself to surf. I'm not supposed to mingle with humans. I only went out on the water when they weren't there. Like at night or in bad weather. I got struck by lightning. It stopped my heart, I went under—and once I was fished out of the ocean, I had to start the healing process all over.

Long story short, it was thanks to a genetic lottery ticket that I reanimated as a "revenant" after death. But it was a technicality that turned me into an evil one instead of a good one. Since I died betraying someone to their death, even though it was Frankie and he totally deserved it, I turned into an evil "numa" instead of a "bardia," the good-guy revenants who repeatedly die saving people's lives.

But I'm not evil. I swear.

Kate, the revenants' Champion, saw my underlying good nature and gave me the chance to redeem myself. Which I did by helping her kill Violette. After that fatal act, Kate asked Bran Tandôrn, a healer, or *"guérisseur,"* to take my corpse to his home on the northwest coast of France and transition me from numa to bardia. Or at least, to try. It hadn't been done for a millennium or so.

When a revenant (good or evil) dies, they come back to life three days later at the age of their original, human death. Remember when I said it was important that my first death was at thirteen? Under the normal rules, I should stay thirteen forever. Which would totally suck. Who in their right mind would want to be stuck in perpetual puberty?

But Bran figured I was a special case. He should know. *Guérisseurs* are rare, but fairly well known in France. And Bran's one of an even smaller group who specialize in healing revenants. They're called Flame-fingers, and he's the one Kate contacted when Paris's bardia needed help. He's been my guardian since Kate entrusted me to his care.

Between the time I got to Brittany and my unfortunate run-in with lightning, I actually aged. I grew a few inches and hair sprouted…everywhere. Which was exhilarating. I wasn't trapped in a child's body, after all. I was beginning to prove Bran's theory that during my transition from numa to bardia, I would age at the same rate as a human. Which was further proved when I woke back up from my lightning-strike death with my age reset at thirteen, shorter and less hairy, the telltale red lines of a numa threading back through my aura. (This especially sucked. They had almost disappeared.)

So, Bran strictly forbade me from dying. And it worked. It's been four years, and now I have the body of a seventeen-year-old. After working out daily and following weapons training videos that Ambrose and Gaspard post on a private server for me, my shoulders are broader, and I have the beginnings of a six-pack. I'm too slim and lanky to ever be as jacked as Ambrose, but I'm…not bad.

Bran assumes my aging will stop when I die as a bardia, saving someone's life. Right now, I don't have the urge to die, like bardia do. And I don't have the craving to betray, like numa do. But I don't sleep and I'm dormant three days a month, so I'm somewhere in between. I'd like to keep it that way for a few more years. See if I get any taller and bulk out a bit. You know…finish growing. Become a little more adult before my default reset age is set in stone. I'm thinking twenty-two seems like a good age to die a fourth time.

Avoiding death wouldn't be a problem if I stay here in Brittany. We're in the middle of the countryside. All cows and sheep and farming and…that's pretty much it. It's officially the most boring, uneventful place on earth. That's what Bran had planned…a few more years of this snoozefest and I would, as he said, "achieve my full potential." But yesterday I got the call. I've been invited to move to Paris. Why? Bran just said that my "bardia kindred" would fill me in. (I always feel uncomfortable when he uses that term, since it isn't technically accurate: I'm not yet a bardia, so I haven't earned the status of "kindred.")

Paris is where I grew up. But this time will be different. The thought of being with people I've basically idolized for the last five years fills my heart with both dread and excitement. I knew Kate a little. I spent a few days weaning her back to life after Violette killed her. But the rest of her kindred I only met on the day of the Final Battle, just before I died and was whisked away to Brittany. Jules and Ava stopped by about three months after I moved in with Bran, but they only stayed a day.

I've begged Bran to tell me everything he knows about Paris's bardia. Googling is useless, because they use aliases when they save lives or do anything in the public eye. So basically, I'm moving in tomorrow with a bunch of undead superheroes who I barely know but secretly worship. And even though I used to be their enemy and haven't technically yet become one of them, they say they want my help.

So…no pressure or anything.

Chapter Two

"Here he is! The lean mean fightin' machine, come all the way from Bumfart Brittany to give me some exercise!"

A man the size of a tank appears in the grand archway of the massive stone Paris mansion the bardia call "La Maison," flinging the doors open before I can get close enough to knock. I have to look up to meet his eyes. Ambrose is about twice as big as I remember him; the training videos do no justice to his sheer bulk.

He throws a meaty arm around my shoulders and squeezes, making me feel like a very fragile pencil. "You don't have to knock, man, you're kindred," he says, pulling me into the foyer, then yells over his shoulder, "Hey baby, look what the Crow dragged in!" He lets go of me and reaches for Bran. (Bran's name means *crow* in Breton, and with his bottle-thick glasses, black, slicked-back hair, ivory skin and sharp nose, the nickname suits him.) My mentor does a fancy sidestep to avoid Ambrose's grasp, and slips past us.

Charlotte is coming down the winding marble staircase, arm in arm with Gaspard, their heads almost touching in what looks like a serious discussion. The last time I saw her, she was dressed in black, wielding a crossbow—a fierce teenage fighter ready to sink bolts into numa heads. Now her blonde hair is pulled back from her peaches and cream complexion and she looks like an older, more responsible version of warrior-Charlotte. That is, until she sees me.

She squeals, "Oh my god! It's Louis!" then takes the rest of the stairs at a run and throws herself on me. "Welcome, kindred. You're finally here. We've been waiting forever!"

"Five years," I say, when I can breathe again.

She holds me back to inspect me, and I self-consciously tuck a stray lock of hair behind my ear. "Look at you. You've grown up! What are you now? Six feet?"

"Six foot two," I reply, embarrassed by the attention.

"Now all we have to do is bulk you out," Ambrose says, squeezing my barely-existent bicep.

I want to find a table to hide under, but Charlotte's still talking. "We would have come to visit you in Brittany, but we weren't allowed."

Ambrose drapes his arm around her and wiggles his ring finger to show off a thick gold band. "We invited you to the wedding."

"Yeah, I know," I say. "I really wanted to be there, but it was just a few months after I arrived at Bran's, and he said I was under lockdown."

"You missed the event of the century. Maybe even the millennium," he muses.

"Don't rub it in," I say. "I spent the last five years in the middle of nowhere with absolutely zero social life."

"What about school?" Charlotte asks.

"Homeschooled."

Ambrose's mouth puckers like he bit a lemon. "Man, that's harsh. Hey, remember that time you got struck by lightning?"

"Um, yeah." I grin. "Kind of hard to forget."

"Well, when Bran called, I had the car out front in seconds, but Gaspard said only Kate and Vincent could go. Kate said she saw your aura from the highway when they were still three hours away."

"Good thing," I say. "My body had floated so far out to sea, they had to borrow a boat to come get me. But by the time I reanimated, they were back in Paris. So even if you had come, I wouldn't have been awake to see you."

"Sounds lonely." Charlotte gives me a look of pity.

Ambrose pats me on the back. "I can't imagine five years with only Bran for company. Don't get me wrong, he's a quality guy. But he acts like a grandpa, and I'm sure you could use some excitement."

Bran, who went out to retrieve a notebook from the car, chooses this moment to return. He clears his throat to indicate he heard what Ambrose said.

"No offense, man, but you know it's true," says Ambrose, unapologetically.

Charlotte has been grinning mischievously, like she's already plotting my future social life. She lunges back in for another smothering hug. Ambrose wraps his arms around both of us.

Gaspard has been standing, hands behind his back, studying this reunion with a slight grin on his lips and eyebrow raised, like he's witnessing a curiosity. Now, he steps around the person-sandwich I've become and gives Bran a couple of formal cheek kisses. His raven black hair makes him look as though his grooming routine is limited to sticking his finger in electrical sockets. "Good to see you, old friend. I assume your journey was without incident?"

"The TGV is a thing of wonder," Bran says. "I would much rather take a high-speed train than maneuver my old station wagon through the streets of Paris."

"And Louis," Gaspard says, turning to me. "You look better than when I saw you last time."

"Less dead," I say.

Gaspard lost his longtime partner, Jean-Baptiste, in the Final Battle. The numa had killed him and burned his body—the only way to permanently destroy a revenant. Even though I barely know Gaspard, I can see how deeply it must have affected him. The lines in his face seem etched by sorrow instead of age.

"How is Louis's aura?" he asks, turning to Bran.

As a Flame-finger, or healer specializing in revenants, Bran can see things we can't. Like auras. Or volant spirits. But I'll get to that later.

He studies the space around my head, which feels weird, but trust me, I've gotten used to it. "The red threads have completely disappeared. But he does not yet have the golden aura of a bardia. That won't happen until his first rescue. He is, I suppose you would say, a blank slate of a revenant."

And there it is. The whole source of my anxiety in a nutshell. I'm not yet one of them. It's a fact. But from the way Charlotte and Ambrose stand, each with an arm around me, they don't seem to care.

"Good, good." Gaspard inspects me like I'm a scientific specimen. Which I guess I am, seeing as I'm the first numa to have "transitioned" during any of their lifetimes.

"You are welcome here, kindred," he says. "We are pleased that you are moving in."

"Thank you," I say, bending in a formal bow before I can catch myself. Ambrose chuckles and my face gets hot. *Where did that come from?* I think. I'm pretty sure I've never bowed in my life. Gaspard brings out the Louis XIV in me.

As he starts up the stairs with Bran, he calls, "Ambrose, would you let everyone know Bran and Louis have arrived and that we will convene in the library?"

"Don't you think Louis needs time to freshen up?" Ambrose asks. "Maybe eat a meal? Get in some training?"

I look between Ambrose and Gaspard and shrug. "I'm actually good."

Gaspard raises an eyebrow at Ambrose. "Apparently, he is good."

Ambrose mumbles something about *just trying to be hospitable* and heads toward the kitchen.

Charlotte takes my arm. "We all know it's Ambrose who wants the meal and the workout. But we should go ahead and discuss what you'll be doing here. After the meeting, you'll have plenty of time to get settled."

She leads me up the stairs toward the library, and I try not to gawk at everything. The crystal chandelier the size of a Volkswagen Beetle hanging over the foyer. The upstairs hallway lined with antique carpets. The marble pedestal holding a vase of fresh flowers that smell like Bran's garden after the rain.

Kate brought me to La Maison, located in a super-posh tree-lined neighborhood in Paris's sixth district, for a few hours before the Final Battle. But I was too shell-shocked from having deserted the group of evil undead who had resurrected me to have the bandwidth to appreciate the decor. Plus, I spent most of that time in a dark room giving intel—filling the bardia in on everything I had witnessed during my months with Violette and the numa.

Now that I know I'm going to stay, I'm hyper-aware of my surroundings, and realize how impressive the house is. It's a *hotel particulier*, a palace inside the city, complete with a garden and hidden behind a high stone enclosure. But it doesn't feel cold and historic, like Violette's castle, where bleakness practically oozed from the cold grey walls. No, this place is warm. It feels alive.

If I'm honest, it seems way too good for me. I know I shouldn't get hung up on it, but I can't help it. However unwillingly, I worked with their enemies. And I haven't even proved myself by saving a human life. So, I don't feel like I deserve to be embraced so warmly. But I want to. Desperately. I'm determined to earn the trust they're investing in me.

In the library, Gaspard and Bran are deep in conversation, seated at a large round oak table surrounded by a dozen chairs. Stacked in the middle are piles of books and a laptop that sticks out like a sore thumb since it's the only electric item in the room besides the lamps.

Although I'm not a big reader, libraries impress me. They have that hushed, holy feeling of churches. This one feels more like a cathedral. Its ceiling towers twenty feet overhead, and there are wooden ladders to access shelves that are too high to reach. The smell of furniture polish hangs in the air, mixed with the odors of old paper and candlewax.

Charlotte and I take chairs across the table from others, not wanting to disturb them. She leans in and says in a hushed voice, "I'm so glad you're here. I feel like I already know you. Kate told me how you helped her escape the houseboat where Violette imprisoned her, and I saw your courage when you turned your back on the numa and joined us. I just want you to know how brave I think you are."

I can tell my face is flushing. I'm not used to this sort of sincerity, and definitely not this type of praise.

"I can see I'm embarrassing you, so I'll stop," she says, leaning back in her chair. "But, you know, I suffered a traumatic childhood like you did. Most of us have some sort of damage in our past. So even though you're new here, and you may not feel you fit in, just know there are things we all share that makes you one of us."

Luckily for my tear ducts, Ambrose takes that moment to burst into the room like the door's too small for him. "Mission accomplished." he announces to Gaspard. "They're on their way." He plops down into the chair next to Charlotte and rubs his hands together in anticipation of the meeting.

Hey kid. I hear the words in my mind and look around in surprise.

Ambrose leans back in his chair to peer at me from behind Charlotte. "Arthur says to say hi. He's flying around here somewhere." He twirls his finger toward the ceiling.

I had almost forgotten about being "volant" since I don't have that ability yet. Most revenants, bardia and numa alike, have two stages of dormancy each month. The first day, they're "mind and body dead." Then, the second and third day, their mind wakes up, and they're "volant," which basically means a ghost. Their body lies there, skin cold, heart stopped, but their spirit can travel, speak telepathically to other revenants, see a few seconds into the future, and (in cases of extreme need) possess the body of another revenant, or even a human, although that's not the best idea. Makes the human go crazy, thus inadvisable.

You can't even imagine how many revenant rules there are. After five years of studying, I still don't know some of them. So yeah, today Arthur's a ghost. "Hi," I say out loud, because, except for with Kate, who has some kind of Champion ESP, the telepathy doesn't go both ways. (That would be Revenant Rules #3,641 and #3,642. Kidding. Kind of.)

You're looking good, he replies. *Seems this afterlife's treating you well.*

"Thanks, Arthur." I feel self-conscious conversing with the air, although from the way everyone ignores me, it's clear they're all used to it. Besides Kate, Arthur's probably the bardia I talked to the most before leaving for Brittany. After the skirmish where I switched sides, Vincent told him to guard me on the walk back to La Maison. He was giving me these weird looks, like he was trying not to laugh. I finally asked, "What?"

"You're Violette's new consort?"

I didn't respond. The word "consort" made it sound like we were a couple, when I was actually just the person she wanted around while she bitched about things and ordered people around.

He patted me on the shoulder and said, "You decided to run away after being with her for six months? You should have tried five hundred years."

I hadn't realized he was *the* Arthur—the one Violette chose me to replace after he turned against her. But once I did, man, I felt bad for him. So, we were able to have that bonding moment before she ordered someone to put an arrow through my head.

Vincent is next through the door. He looks the same as he did five years ago. That dark, handsome, brooding look, like the tortured hero of a graphic novel. His eyes meet mine and he frowns.

My stomach twists into a knot as he walks up to me. I force myself to stand and shake his hand. "Welcome," he says. Everyone looks up, waiting, but he doesn't say anything else. The omission makes it clear: He doesn't see me as kindred. Just as I had feared.

When Kate offered me amnesty during the skirmish, Vincent was against it. He had knocked me to the ground and was about to run his sword through me when Kate stopped him. And though I fought side-by-side with her after that, he still didn't trust me. He had me tell him my story as we walked back to La Maison, and afterward I overheard him say to Kate that even though my case was "different," my destiny had been decided. Once a numa always a numa, even if it wasn't fair. Kate defied him, and he finally caved.

I proved whose side I was on when I threw the knife at Violette, but even that didn't win him over. For the last five years, he's kept his silence. I'd wondered if, over time, he'd changed his opinion of me. Now the answer's clear.

He takes the chair next to Bran and leans in to listen to what others are discussing. I must look as uncomfortable as I feel, because Charlotte pats me on the arm and whispers, "Don't take it personally. Vincent'll come around."

So, I'm in a pretty shitty frame of mind when Kate enters the room and wipes every dark thought from my mind. She looks exactly the same as the last time I saw her, which I suppose is normal since she has probably died several times since then, always coming back at seventeen. Her eyes zoom in on me. She smiles broadly, and it's like a floodlight is switched on in the room. I can't help but stand up and walk over to her. She opens her arms wide, and I step in for the best hug ever. I know it's genuine, and it feels earned. We've both saved each other's lives. Several times. Nothing works for bonding like repeatedly rescuing someone from the brink of death.

She holds me back, looks me in the eyes and says, "Welcome, kindred."

Chapter Three

No one speaks for a moment, until Ambrose says, "I hate to break up this touching reunion, but for those of us who have short attention spans and big appetites, could it continue *after* the meeting?"

"Ambrose!" Charlotte scolds.

"What?" he asks. "Jeanne put madeleines in the oven and they're probably ready by now."

"Yes, let us begin," Gaspard says. I sit back down next to Charlotte. Kate takes the chair between me and Vincent, laying her hand gently on his and leaning in to kiss him. There's still the same electricity between them that I witnessed five years ago. Like their pure delight in being together hasn't faded over time. All of the doubt and darkness Vincent radiated when he spotted me disappears in the light of Kate's positivity. She softens his rough edges. I'm glad she's sitting between us.

Gaspard begins the meeting, threading his fingers together and leaning forward to address the table. "To bring Louis up to date, numa activity has returned to Paris."

"Wait, what?" My heart drops and my hands get clammy. To be honest, the only reason I felt comfortable coming to Paris was knowing there weren't any numa left. "I thought you ran them off years ago!"

"Not just ran them off. We also killed them," Ambrose boasts.

"It's true," Gaspard says. "For a couple of years after the Final Battle, there was relative peace."

"Our contacts in the Paris police force couldn't understood why crime rates dropped so dramatically," Charlotte says with a wry smile. "Of course, the French government took all the credit."

Vincent clarifies. "Drugs, prostitution, murder, corruption, money-laundering, those were still around. But, *as you well know*, the numa have always been the kingpins of the underworld. And with them gone, only a few humans were left to run the show."

I didn't miss the *as you well know* jab. Neither did Kate, who shifted closer to me.

"However, businesses previously owned by numa have recently been reopening," Gaspard continues. "They're using different names but have the same human managers and suppliers as before. We suspect Paris's numa have relaunched their activities from somewhere farther outside the city."

"I can still see numa auras from a distance," Kate confirms, "so I'm one hundred percent sure none are physically present in Paris."

"But get this. Two days ago," Charlotte says, "Ambrose and I were on patrol with Henri, one of our kindred, who was volant. We were doing surveillance on a reopened numa bar—used to be called Judas. While we were checking it out, we were attacked by humans acting suspiciously like numa."

"What do you mean?" I ask.

"First of all, they used numa strategy," she responds. "One distracted Henri so he wouldn't see the others coming. Then the other two attacked us."

"We fought them off, of course," Ambrose says, as if it were nothing.

Charlotte rolls her eyes. "These guys were huge. And crazy violent. They had sword skills like trained numa. Two got away. Ambrose knocked the other out. We tried to bring him back for questioning, but he regained consciousness in the car and escaped."

"Not before I got a picture of his tats," Ambrose says.

Kate pulls a photo up on the laptop. She positions the screen so both I and Bran can see. It's a close-up shot of a tattoo. Next to the letters "N.A." is a symbol that looks like a swastika missing one arm.

Bran leans back. "Yes, you sent me that image. I have seen nothing like that in the symbols of my people…or elsewhere."

"What's it stand for?" I ask.

"Well, just before they ran off, one of the guys yelled, 'Numa Army,'" Charlotte says.

"Thus the N.A.," I say. "And they were human?"

"Definitely," Charlotte confirms.

I look around at the group. "So, the numa have a human army?"

"It seems that way," Gaspard says.

"That was our first contact with them," Charlotte says. "Of course, the goal is to find the rest—if there are others—and get them to talk."

"How are you going to do that?" I ask.

"Well, I suggested infiltrating them," Vincent says.

"They'd know you were bardia right away," I respond.

"That's why one of *us* can't do it." He raises an eyebrow.

It feels like he dumped a bucket of ice-cold water over my head. "Um...me?" I croak, but the words don't quite come out because my throat has squeezed shut.

"That's *not* what we're asking," Kate says quickly. She turns to Vincent. "Like I said, that idea is a non-starter. It would be extremely problematic for us to ask Louis to go back to the numa, after he showed such courage to leave."

"He's the only chance we have to get in there," Vincent argues. "The numa don't know for sure what happened to him. And it would be in their character to believe he would betray us and return to them."

I wrap my arms around my chest and try not to freak out. I shoot a glance across the table at Bran. Saying he looks concerned would be an understatement.

"I was under the impression that Louis was to provide insight into the numa so that you could track down their followers. Not to infiltrate. It's too soon. His psychic wounds are still fresh," Bran says.

"But he's not a bardia," Vincent argues. "You just said it—he's a blank slate."

"Perhaps," Bran says, considering. "But I haven't prepared him for interacting with the numa. I didn't think there would be any need...any time soon, at least. And I had hoped you would afford him more time to...well, to grow into his full potential, physically, before there might be a need for him to reanimate as a bardia."

Is it possible to be in the midst of a panic attack and simultaneously die of humiliation? Because if so, that's exactly what I'm doing right now.

Kate places her hand on mine. "We're not talking about Louis reanimating quite yet," she insists, "or infiltrating the numa. I am vehemently against that idea." She turns to me. "I won't put you at risk. I know your heart is good, but they could entrap you. All we're asking you is to help us think like the numa, remember the places they took you, any information you might have that could help us." She glances around the room. "We're agreed on that, right?"

Everyone nods, except Vincent.

Reassured, she turns to me. "But that's just part of the reason we need you here now. Gaspard and Bran have decided it's time for you to take on your role as our representative."

My mind is spinning. We were just discussing whether or not I would have to face my biggest nightmare—going back to the numa—and now Kate's talking about…"I'm sorry, what?" I ask.

"Your role representing France's bardia." She holds a hand up as I begin to protest. "And, yes, you can start even before technically becoming one of us. I have always trusted you. So, when we chose our representative in the new bardia-Flame-finger partnership, you were the first person I thought of."

I glance at Bran and Gaspard. "I thought the two of you represent the Flame-fingers and bardia. You've been working together for five years."

"We're just stuffy old researchers," Bran replies, "comparing ancient manuscripts. To take the partnership forward, we need two of the younger generation. People who understand today's world."

"You mean who can use a computer?" Ambrose nudges Gaspard, who rolls his eyes but cracks an almost invisible smile.

Bran chuckles. "That, and more. People who don't live in the past."

Kate chimes in. "You are a bardia—or you will be one day—and you've been living with a Flame-finger for the last five years. Bran's been telling you about their ways, so you surely understand them better than any of us. Believe me, you're the perfect choice."

This is a lot of information for one day. I wonder if I'm capable of living up to their expectations. It sounds intimidating to say the least.

"So?" Kate asks.

I swallow the lump in my throat. "I accept. Of course. You know I'll do anything you ask."

"Well, that's just great!" Ambrose rubs his hands together as he rises. "I propose we all move down to the kitchen for some celebratory snacks."

"Sorry," Bran says. "Louis and I need to be on our way." He turns to me. "I'll take you to Le Corbeau to meet your Flame-finger counterpart, then you can come back and get moved in."

"Wait, you've already chosen someone for your side?" I wonder how many other secrets my mentor has been hiding from me.

"I'm sure you'll get along," Bran says. "He's a lot like me."

Ambrose shakes his head. "Not at all like you."

Bran says, "Well, of course not *exactly* like me, seeing as he's eighteen."

"Still nothing like you," Ambrose says. "No offense." He reaches out to give him a side-hug that Bran immediately wriggles out of. Ambrose winks at me to show he knows how much Bran hates hugging and that that's actually the whole point.

Chapter Four

As I step through the door of Bran's family's antiques and reliquary shop, the smell of incense transports me back to the day five years ago when Violette brought me here, accompanied by two of her goons and the disembodied spirit of Vincent. We charged down the stairs to the basement, where just hours before my "colleagues" had killed Bran's mother and left him tied him up for questioning. But by the time we arrived, Kate and Georgia had rescued Bran and disappeared.

When Bran and I talked through my entire numa history, back when I first got to Brittany, he gave me his version of the story. Him, beat up, gagged and duct-taped to a chair in the basement. Kate and Georgia arriving and releasing him. The three of them escaping through a basement access to the Paris sewers just as Violette and I arrived.

I told him my version: Violette throwing a screaming fit until the two thugs broke through the barred door and charged into the sewer tunnels to search for them. Too late. I cowered while Violette ranted and raved and smashed things against the wall.

It's that helpless feeling that I remember now, frighteningly similar to what I felt when I watched Frankie beat up my mom and siblings. I didn't do anything—until finally I did, and then it was the wrong thing. Remorse slams me like a wrecking ball, and I stop, unable to walk further into a place filled with such dark memories.

Bran studies my face and sees what's going on in my head. "You're a different person now," he says.

I lean over and prop my hands on my knees until my head stops swimming.

Bran and I have talked about everything. My numa life and before. It was part of my therapy. "A process of absolution," Bran called it. Talking through it meant facing the bad things I did, or at least witnessed and didn't actively try to stop. It was supposed to help me feel forgiveness from something bigger than myself. From God, the universe, take your pick.

Bran said I had post-traumatic stress. The fact that the evil had scarred me emotionally was further proof I was never meant to be a numa. I thought all that pain and mental turmoil was over. But now, standing in the place where bad shit went down and knowing the numa were out there again…it's hitting me all over again.

"I'm sorry," I say. "It's the memories."

Bran sits me down and waits until I'm looking him in the eyes. "Everything that happened is firmly in the past. This is a new start for you, Louis. You're clean. Very few have gotten that chance. And I know you'll make the most of it."

I inhale deeply through my nose and let it escape through my lips, the technique Bran taught me to calm panic. "I'm going to make up for everything I did…and didn't do," I say finally.

"I know."

"Is that you, *Tonton* Bran?" calls a voice from the back of the store.

I'm on my feet in an instant, knocking the chair over in my alarm. Bran lays a hand on my shoulder. "It's okay."

I hear footsteps on the stairway leading down from Bran's Paris apartment, and a boy emerges through the door. As he walks toward us, I see he's my age. My height. Black curly hair cropped short. Brown skin glowing bronze under the dim light. On his forearm is a tattoo of a flaming triangle inside a circle. I recognize it. It's the *signum bardia*, a symbol given to humans the bardia trust. He must be a Flame-finger like Bran.

He gives Bran a back-thumping hug, which, unlike with Ambrose, Bran accepts, probably because it's not squeezing the life out of him. Also, if the guy called him *tonton* or "uncle," he's family. "Welcome back!" the boy says, then turns to me. "So you must be my immortal counterpart!"

At least, that's what I think he says. Because as our eyes meet, my ears stop working, along with the rest of my body. Except for my heart, which flops around in my chest like a fish on dry land.

Bran and the boy wait for me to say something, but my mouth is on sympathy strike with the rest of my body, so I just stand there like an idiot.

One side of the boy's lips quirks up. "I'm Siaka."

"Louis," I manage to get out.

Then he does what any normal French person would do when they meet a friend of a friend. He leans in to give me a quick peck on each cheek. In spite of it being a totally innocent gesture, when his face brushes mine, my skin flames and my ears burn.

Oh, god, please don't let me blush.

Luckily Bran starts talking, so when we step back from our introductory cheek-kisses, I focus on my mentor and not on the boy who caused my body's all-out revolution.

"Siaka's father is my cousin on my mother's side, from Brittany. And his mother's family are well-known *guérisseurs* from Mali. They are the most ancient line of Flame-fingers in that land."

I nod, still avoiding Siaka's eyes. I touch two fingers to my cheek, pretending I'm scratching it. My skin is on fire.

"And Louis is—" Bran begins.

Siaka cuts him off. "Yeah, I've heard about you."

I can't help looking at him now. How much does he know?

"We study you guys, since revenants are our specialty topic." He smiles again. It's a nice, friendly smile, totally open. I breathe a sigh of relief. He must not have noticed my temporary paralysis.

"I heard you betrayed your abusive, drug-dealing stepdad and got him killed by his supplier. That was fierce! I totally would have done the same thing."

"Siaka!" Bran sounds shocked.

"What?" Siaka looks at Bran, a challenge in his eyes. "That was the brave thing to do. He was protecting his mom and siblings."

"He could have gone to the police instead," suggests Bran.

"Like *they* would have done anything," said Siaka, a tone of bitterness beneath his words. He tears his gaze from Bran and nods at me. "Respect!"

"Thanks," I say uncomfortably.

"It just sucks that it got you turned into a numa. But hey, it's all good now, right?"

"I still feel pretty bad about a lot of things." I throw Bran a glance.

"Well, now you're back. You have all the time in the world to make things right," Siaka says.

This time, I'm able to look him in the eyes. "That's exactly what I plan to do."

The smile he gives me in return seems to say so many different things that I don't know how to interpret it.

It definitely says, "I respect you." It seems to say, "Oh man, we're going to be really good friends." But I very much doubt it's saying what I want it to say: "Yeah, I like you too."

***

"Let's get to work," Siaka says, and leads us down the back stairs to the basement.

"Wow! This place has changed!" I gape around at the brightly lit space. What was a dark storage space for antiques five years ago is now a fully-fledged laboratory. Metal tables hold scientific equipment, a counter with sinks lines one wall, and a ventilation system turns on when Siaka flicks a switch, sucking stale air from the basement and blowing it out through vents near the ceiling.

"This is where old meets new." Bran gestures proudly at his lab. "You know I've been getting in touch with other Flame-fingers worldwide, asking them to send me all the revenant-related information they find in their families' documents or oral stories. Some of those contain formulas and cures, and this is where I'm attempting to recreate them, with the invaluable help of my master-chemist, Siaka."

Siaka chuckles and shakes his head. "I'm just a First Year in chemistry at the Sorbonne. I've got a long way to go before I'm master of anything!"

"He's being modest," Bran reassures me.

"Yeah, well, I watched my mom practice her craft when I was a kid, so I learned about healing from her. I'm studying chemistry to learn how science might explain, and maybe even amp up the effects."

"Is your mom on board with that?" I ask, wondering what healers like Bran feel about someone trying to quantify, or even improve upon, their gift.

Siaka shuffles a few bottles around, keeping his eyes on the table. "My mother died last year."

Oh shit. I put my foot in it there, bringing up a painful topic ten minutes after meeting him. I feel like telling him I'm an asshole but settle for, "I'm sorry."

He accepts it with a nod and forces himself to meet my eyes. "Breast cancer. She could heal other people, but not herself." He clears his throat. "She passed me the gift before she died. Do you know how that works?"

"Yeah, Bran told me. Only one person in a *guérriseur* family has 'the gift.' When they decide they're done using it, they can transfer it to a willing member of the family. But only a very few *guérriseur* families are Flame-fingers—able to heal revenants as well as humans."

Siaka grins. "Sounds like you've been studying us as much as we've studied you."

"Hoping that Louis would take the role as bardia ambassador," Bran says, "I've trusted him with more of our secrets than any of his kindred … including Gaspard." He pulls a bunch of leaves out of his bag and piles them on the table. "The moleweed I promised you from the cliffs near my house." He and Siaka begin stripping leaves off their stalks to place in a colander.

"So, what exactly are you working on here?" I ask, relieved to change the subject.

"It's a three-step process," Siaka says. "One: we recreate the formula. Two: we test it on bardia volunteers. And three: if it works, I do a chemical analysis to understand *why* it works and if substitutes can be used for rare ingredients. That way the formulas will be easier to reproduce."

"It's all working toward the goal of information sharing," Bran adds. "Thanks to a communication platform set up by Siaka, we are linking the global community of Flame-fingers online, as your bardia have already done with their Worldwide Consortium."

"Most Flame-fingers lost contact with each other centuries ago," Siaka says. "It hasn't been easy to get a global network set up."

"This is a project you'll be working on together." Bran looks up from his leaf-stripping. "Gaspard has given you control of the bardia's database, Louis. When Siaka's ready, you can link the two on a shared platform."

"That way, our people across the world can replicate Bran's and my experiments," Siaka says, "and make suggestions based on their culture and traditions. The bardia will test our cures. Everyone reports their outcomes on the platform, and from there we make changes – tweak, test more, until we get results!"

"So, our job is to centralize the global research between Flame-fingers and bardia?"

"It's the most effective way to communicate and share information that Gaspard and I could come up with," Bran admits.

"Sounds genius." I turn to Siaka. "So, you're a chemist *and* a programmer?"

"Actually, someone else is helping me with the tech stuff." He chuckles, and I try to ignore how soft his lips look against his perfect white teeth.

Bran watches us with an amused smile.

"What?" I ask.

"It's just that…you two are the faces of the new generation. You symbolize the union between our people. I can't help but feel I'm witnessing a ground-breaking moment."

Siaka's eyes meet mine, and the realization dawns. We're tasked with the historical reunion of ancient allies. A reunion that could change the world.

"I don't mind being the poster boy for Flame-fingers. How about you?" Siaka challenges.

"Representing a clan of walking dead superheroes?" I smile. "Why not?"

Chapter Five

"Feeling kind of useless." Bran and Siaka are doing things with bottles and plants and instruments while I sit here like a lump. Now, with the ice broken, I don't feel quite as awkward around Siaka. It's nice to hang out with someone my age for once, even if Bran's here with us.

"Take this." Siaka hands me what looks like an ancient manuscript. Words are handwritten in cryptic letters on a page of stretched animal skin. It feels as though it could fall apart if I breathe the wrong way. The mildew odor suggests it was buried underground for eons and only recently dug up.

"It's seventeenth century," Bran comments.

"I can smell that."

Siaka laughs. "We received it last week from a Flame-finger family near Stonehenge."

I scan the weird calligraphy, attempting to decipher the words. "Um, my English is pretty good, but I'm not sure I understand monk-speak or whatever this is."

"Give it a try," Siaka encourages.

I tip the parchment toward the light. "'Thou shalt take a mortar and pestle made of the finest granite dug from the dark depths of the earth.' I glance up. 'What the…?"

"That would be these," says Siaka, holding up a stone bowl and one of those crushing-sticks like you see in the windows of old-timey pharmacies. Mortar and pestle? I think that's what they're called.

"Did you dig these from the dark depths of the earth?" I ask, trying to look serious.

He laughs. "Someone must have."

"Okay, then." I continue to read. "Thou shalt crush ten leaves of the moleweed plant, harvested under the beams of a full moon with scissors crafted from the finest silver."

"Check," says Bran, counting out ten of the leaves.

"Wait a minute. Did you seriously harvest those with silver scissors under a full moon?"

"Yes," Bran says. "That's why I was out all night last Wednesday."

"Where do you even find silver scissors?"

"They're antiques. I have two sets upstairs for sale," he says.

"Are you guys actually following all of these crazy mystical rules scribbled down by ancient medicine men?" I ask.

"We haven't changed our techniques much in the last millennium," says Siaka, cracking a smile. "So, you're basically talking to two medicine men who follow crazy mystical rules on a regular basis."

"Oops." I'm embarrassed but also kind of in awe. There's so much more to Bran and Siaka than meets the eye.

"To be honest," Siaka says, "we're following every rule, however weird it sounds. Who knows, maybe silver has a chemical effect on moleweed? And farmers have been planting and harvesting their crops based on phases of the moon for millennia. Now they just make it sound hip by calling it 'biodynamic.' There's so much we still don't understand about science. So, if our ancestors stumbled upon something that worked, we replicate their instructions to the letter."

They work in silence for a moment before Siaka catches my eye. "Even so, if the formula succeeds, I'll test it again with easier-to-find objects, like regular pruning shears from a garden shop ... see if we get the same results. The simpler we make the formulas, the easier it'll be for our kindred to recreate them wherever they are in the world."

I'm feeling pretty intimidated by how much Siaka already knows at eighteen years of age. But I'm distracted from that thought when Bran drops the leaves into the bowl and Siaka starts crushing them, and I can't stop watching the movement of his bicep as he grinds the leaves.

He looks up, as though he's sensed me watching.

"Um...cool?" I say, which sounds majorly stupid after his whole cultural history speech.

He raises an eyebrow.

"What?" I ask, all deer-in-headlights.

"What comes next?" he prompts.

"Oh! Yeah." I pick the manuscript up. Bran's fooling around with some bottles over a sink, so he doesn't witness me blushing. Again.

"When the leaves of the moleweed plant are crushed into the finest of powder, thou shalt sprinkle it with forty tears wept by a revenant and mix into a thick paste." I jerk my head up. "Wait a minute...the *tears* of a revenant?"

Siaka puts down the crusher and digs through his backpack. He pulls out a vial of clear liquid and hands it to Bran.

"What the…?" I begin. "That can't be."

"It can," Bran replies, pouring the liquid into the bowl.

"Where in the world did you get that many tears from a revenant?"

"Charlotte volunteered her husband for the task," Siaka says.

I stare at him.

"Sad movies," he says, shrugging. "Ambrose is a sucker for them. I showed him *Titanic* followed by *The Notebook*. By the time we got through *Old Yeller*, he was ugly crying and I got two test tubes worth, so we have a back stock." Siaka says this totally straight-faced, but when he looks up at me from the bowl, we both start laughing.

Even Bran chuckles. "Stop it!" he scolds. "I'm measuring."

Half an hour later we've added "the milk of a goat who has birthed three kids" (which necessitated Bran visiting several local farmers) and "crushed marble from a widow's tombstone." They heated the concoction over "an open flame" and poured it into a "vial made of glass blown by a daughter of Eve."

"I bought the vial from Claire, the glassblower living in the artist colony inland from my house," Bran explains. Fitting the top carefully over the glass tube, he says, "We'll give this to Arthur once he's awake."

"Arthur?" I ask.

"He offered to be the guinea pig for this particular experiment." Bran takes off his apron and hangs it on a peg.

"He's trying to see how long he can resist dying," Siaka says. "Which might come in handy if he and your Champion's sister manage to make things work for longer than a few weeks at a time." He winks at me.

I figure he's talking about Georgia, Kate's sister, who I've heard of but haven't met. "You already know everyone at La Maison?" I ask.

"I'm Bran's messenger boy when he's not in town," Siaka says.

"Ha! You're hardly that," Bran says. "Despite our age difference, we are equals. Both fully-fledged Flame-fingers, the sole holder of our respective family's gift."

"Yeah, but you've had the job longer than I have." Siaka nudges his uncle playfully.

"I will grant you that. But you already know so much that by the time you're my age you will have surpassed my knowledge by far."

"We'll see about that, *Tonton*," Siaka says.

"You'd better be off, Louis," Bran says. "I told the kindred I wouldn't keep you long. Charlotte wanted you to patrol with her. I'll stop by La Maison tomorrow to see how you're getting settled."

"I'll go with Louis," Siaka says. "I've got a class tonight. And since you just got back, I'm sure you want me out of your hair."

"I do have some correspondence to catch up on," Bran admits. "Why don't you go ahead, and I'll clean up here."

That seems to suit Siaka, who takes one look at the mess they've made and tells me, "I'll get my jacket from upstairs and meet you out front."

He sprints up the stairs, and I hang back to say goodbye to Bran, who is washing the mortar and pestle in an aluminum sink. The hot water sends up a cloud of steam that hovers in the air like an omen. "I'm glad to see that you and Siaka get along," he says.

"The alliance I formed with Gaspard and the others will not only continue but thrive with your generation. I'll return to Brittany soon to let you get settled without hovering around and smothering you."

"You don't have to," I say. "But I'm honored you trust me."

"I'm honored I had these five years to work with you." Suddenly, he looks at me – not in the eyes, but a few inches away from my head, which means he's studying my aura. "You have a good heart. That's never been in question. Now, what you do with all of that potential…well, that remains to be seen."

He means it as a compliment. But I know him well enough by now to catch the slight note of apprehension in his voice.

"What is it?" I ask.

He sighs. "There are a few who still doubt you can fully convert into a bardia. That the remnants of numa are gone. We'll just have to show them that they're wrong."

Um. What? I knew Vincent wasn't my biggest fan, but there were others who doubted me? The thought makes me feel queasy. "I'll be on my best behavior," I promise.

Bran clasps my shoulder as he looks me straight in the eye. "I know you will."

Chapter Six

Siaka is waiting for me outside the front door. My breath catches when I see him. His black leather jacket stretches tight across his shoulders, and under it is a soft grey T-shirt and blue jeans. He's so handsome, like movie star handsome, and though I try to keep my cool, I know I'm staring.

He smiles and holds up a helmet.

"You have a motorcycle?" I ask.

"Not quite." He nods to a red scooter parked across the street.

"No way! A vintage Vespa!"

"Yeah, I'm pretty in love with it. I found it in the garage at La Maison. It used to be Vincent's. He said he took Kate out with it on one of their first dates. It was a bit banged up, so I put some time and money into fixing it."

He opens the seat compartment and takes out a second helmet. "Want a ride home?"

"Um, that's a definite yes." I fit the helmet over my head but struggle with the chin strap.

"Let me," Siaka says. As he clicks the strap ends together, his fingers brush my neck, giving me a full-body shudder.

His eyebrows pop up. "Sorry. I should be more careful."

"What do you mean?"

"The Flame-finger-revenant surge thing," he says, grinning.

And then I remember. When Bran placed his hands on me to heal me, it caused something like an electrical current to run through my body. But now, instead of being a not-at-all-attractive older man, it's a totally hot teenage boy. Who's looking at me with an expression of amusement. I wonder if he can see auras like Bran can, and if so, what mine is doing right now. Because my whole body feels like it's sparking with high current voltage.

Now that he's so close, I realize he's slightly taller than me. His jade green eyes are accented by his brown skin. He smells like a mix of peppermint and a Brittany beach roasting in the sun. And his lips, well…I have to look away.

"Are you okay?" he asks.

"Yeah. That *guérriseur*-revenant skin shock…I didn't know it was a thing, besides when Bran was healing me."

"Yeah, I discovered it when I met your kindred at La Maison. I practically electrocuted them all the first time we gave each other the *bises*. Bran told me that when he met Jean-Baptiste, the contact knocked him out. That's actually how he became the Victor Seer: the Flame-finger connection with the head of France's revenants awoke it in him."

"Do you not feel it?" I ask.

He gives me a curious look. "Not usually." But before I can figure out whatever the hell that means, he turns to walk toward the Vespa.

He pulls his phone out of his pocket and taps it. "*Oui, allô?* Sure—I can drop by. Perfect timing, in fact. See you in a minute."

He straddles the scooter and flips up the kickstand. "That's Liv—the one helping me with the Flame-finger database. She wants me to stop by."

My heart drops, and I realize how much I was looking forward to the Vespa ride. "That's okay," I say. "I can take the Métro."

"No, come with me," he says. "I mean, if you want to. You guys can speak Klingon together, or whatever techies speak."

I open my eyes wide, fake-offended. "Hey, I'm slightly techie, but not a fully-qualified geek."

His lips quirk up on one side. "Then answer me this…Star Trek or Star Wars?"

"Star Wars IV, V and VI," I say, without missing a beat. "Forget about I, II and III. And everything that came after is just a nostalgia-bait money grab."

He pats the seat behind him. "You're cool," he concedes. "You can ride."

I climb on and, feeling too awkward to put my hands around his waist, grab on to the seat behind me. Even so, when my knees press his thighs, I'm electrocuted again, but this time I'm expecting it.

"Ready?" he yells through his visor.

"Let's go!" I yell back.

We shoot off down the maze of tiny one-way streets, the motor whining like a mosquito on steroids. My chest is so full of joy that I feel like whooping. I close my eyes and feel the excitement buzz around inside me.

I was thirteen when I left Paris. I always took the city for granted. It was where I was born and raised. Until this moment, I never understood what people meant when they called it magical. But now, speeding through the streets on a sun-soaked May afternoon, I feel like we've broken through a barrier into an alternate universe. The air seems to pop and spark with sorcery.

We pass a woman and her child coming out of a bakery, and the heady smell of freshly baked bread puts me in serious danger of falling off the scooter. We drive past a park where every inch of grass is claimed by people stretched out reading, chatting, flirting, kissing. We speed by a fountain splashing in the middle of a square, and the light catches the water droplets and morphs them into diamonds. Riding through this beautiful city behind this beautiful boy makes me feel like a poet. I want to capture this feeling and express it in transcendent words.

I wonder if this thrill is what love feels like. I've never been in love. When I was in school, I had a couple of crushes, but the boys of interest (it's never been girls…that issue is pretty clear) never knew. I haven't really met anyone since then; Bran and I were so isolated. But now I'm sitting behind this totally hot guy in the most romantic city on earth and everything's beautiful and exciting and we're going to be working together so I'll get to see him all the time and…

Oh my god. I can't like him. The realization dawns on me as he turns the handlebars to drive along the Seine. The sun's glare off the river blinds me. We're going to be *working* together. Representing our people—the Flame-fingers and the bardia. This whole project is based on our relationship. And the bardia are counting on me to prove myself. (Except for those expecting me to fail.) I can't like Siaka—no one will take me seriously if I do.

That's not even considering the probability of unrequited love. Percentage-wise, chances are he's straight. Even if fate is smiling on me and he does like guys, someone that hot definitely has a boyfriend. And even if he doesn't, and he ended up liking me back, and we had an actual relationship, what if we broke up? What if it hurt to even see him, but we had to because our two clans depended on us to represent them? Maybe he wouldn't even want to work with me anymore, and I would fail the very kindred who had given me a second chance and trusted me to help them. My stomach turns, and my throat clenches. That would be a disaster.

I remember my sister calling me a drama queen, and my mother saying, "Louis, you're making a mountain out of a molehill." So I tend to overthink things. But this time, my alarm is justified. A relationship with Siaka is something I can't let happen. We can work together. We can even be friends. But it can't be more.

By the time he pulls the Vespa up to a ramshackle building overlooking the Canal d'Ourc, I have shoved every trace of romance out of my heart. All the fuzzy, delicious cotton candy has left my brain. I am clear of dreams and hopes and anything else that could put my mission at risk. When we pull off our helmets and he play-punches me on the shoulder and says, "Hey, look, you're still in one piece," I barely feel the electricity in his touch. I can't let myself.

Chapter Seven

The building's front entrance is boarded up, as are several of the windows. It looks like no one's used it in decades.

"Wow, what is this place?" I ask.

We walk around the side of the building, let ourselves in through a gate, and cross a courtyard strewn with junky lawn furniture. A couple of rusty chairs are occupied by burnout guys smoking a joint and staring at us like we're the pot police.

"*Salut*," Siaka calls.

"*Ta mère*," one replies. The other laughs like it's the funniest thing he's ever heard.

"Idiots," I murmur.

Siaka ignores them. "To answer your question, the building's a squat." He pulls the door open, letting me into a darkened hallway. A potted plant languishes in one corner, and the elevator is propped open by a two-by-four. "Artists take over vacant buildings that are scheduled to be destroyed. They inform the city of Paris that they are squatting, and the authorities almost always let them stay. It's like a semi-formal contract—the artists pay for electricity and water until the place is torn down, then they move on to another place."

He leads us to a stairwell, and we start the climb. Luckily there's a skylight at the very top: all the lights are burned out. I shield my nose from the sickening smell of body odor and melted plastic.

"And, um, why is your tech person squatting here?" I ask.

"Livia? She's basically a genius: skipped a few grades, graduated early, laughed at the idea of university. Now at sixteen she does freelance work for big corporations and makes bank."

"She can't afford something better than this?" I ask, feeling it in my calves as we pass the fourth floor and head towards the fifth.

"Sure, she can afford it. But she's a hacker. This place gives her street cred."

He pushes open a swinging door, and we emerge into a cavernous loft with widely spaced concrete columns.

The tenants have divided the area into randomly sized zones, each with different decor, like a dozen different mini-worlds packed side-by-side under a ceiling crisscrossed by broken florescent tubes. Trash lines the base of the exterior walls—soda cans, candy wrappers, huge puffballs of dust—like someone swept everything out of the middle of the room but didn't bother to use a dustpan and pick it up.

In one corner, a guy is using an airbrush on a huge canvas to paint graffiti-style art. Against a window, a girl sits at a table behind a sewing machine, attaching a giant piece of silvery plastic to fake leopard fur. Next to her, a metal clothes rack holds several finished garments that look like costumes from the Hunger Games.

A dozen couches are scattered around the space, a person draped across each one, sleeping or meditating or whatever. We weave our way through the obstacle course towards a semi-circle fortress of desks piled with computers and screens and a ton of crap like bobblehead dolls, Lego Millennium Falcons and junk food wrappers. The wall behind it is hung with a *V for Vendetta* poster featuring the creepy "Anonymous" mask and a *Matrix* poster. Life-sized cardboard figures of Neo and Trinity guard the setup on either side. And in the middle of it all sits a girl wearing chunky headphones over an orange knit cap, typing into a keyboard in front of an old-style box computer screen.

"Livia," calls Siaka.

She keeps typing.

We walk right up. Siaka taps her on the shoulder.

She jumps up, rips off her headphones, and turns to face us, looking well and truly pissed off. Black braids drape down past her shoulders. Her skin is a shade lighter than Siaka's and her eyes catlike without the help of liquid liner. She's the classical example of "gorgeous but trying hard not to be."

"Dude!" she yells at Siaka. "Do not do that. Ever."

"I called your name, but you didn't hear me," Siaka says, chuckling.

She turns to me, and her scowl deepens. "Who the hell is this," she asks, looking at me but addressing Siaka.

"This is Louis. I'm working with him on that project you're helping me with."

She glares up at Siaka, who's about a foot taller than her. "What did I say about bringing people here? No visitors. None. Ever."

"Yeah, well, Louis's my work partner, so that's different."

"No. Not different. He is a person, right? And I told you not to bring *people* here. Dude, I've got so much illegal shit on this computer, I could go to jail for the rest of my lifetime… and yours."

"Livia, if you're so concerned about secrecy, why are you working in an open-plan squat with a ton of other people?"

"Okay, first of all, I told you not to call me that. My name is Liv."

Siaka is unfazed. "I've called you Livia since you were a baby."

He turns to me. "Our moms are sisters." I must look confused because he specifies, "My dad's white, hers is Vietnamese."

"Do you really need to do that?" she says, scowling at Siaka. "I'm sure this rando guy doesn't need our family tree explained in detail to figure out why we look nothing alike."

"You actually do look a little…" I begin.

She lifts an eyebrow.

I cave. "Okay, fine. No resemblance."

"Her hacker name is Legacy," Siaka says proudly, earning himself an eye roll.

"Are you the Legacy who hacked into the CRS database and exposed how many of Paris's riot police have criminal records?" I sound like a fanboy, but even among dabblers like me, Legacy is a legend.

She studies my face as if it were a complicated line of coding. "Possibly," she replies. Then repositioning her headphones over her hat, she slumps back into her chair and resumes typing.

Siaka shakes his head at me, and then carefully, as if she's a rattlesnake and not a teenage girl, lifts up the edge of an earphone. "I believe you asked me to stop by. Was there something you wanted to tell me?"

"Not in front of him." Her eyes don't leave her screen.

"Hey, I think I'll check out the garbage bag clothes," I say, glancing toward the girl with the sewing machine.

"No," Siaka insists, draping his arm around my shoulders. I try to ignore the thrill—whether Flame-finger or just hot guy-generated—that courses through my body. "Louis's staying right here. Like I said, I'm working with him now. The database you and I are building will be linked to one he's moderating. He's a part of this conversation."

Liv-slash-Livia-slash-Legacy slips off her headphones and sets them on the desk as though it pains her to do so. She swivels in her chair to face us, crossing her arms and frowning. "I assume that means he's one of *them*."

"Yes," Siaka confirms.

She sighs, like this conversation is costing her so much energy she has none left to breathe. She stares at her cousin from beneath heavy lids. "I wanted to show you the hub. It's basically like WhatsApp, Facebook and Zoom combined. Each member has a profile and can leave updates, communicate by phone, text, or video, and hold video meetings with shared desktop and document capabilities. It has a Dropbox-style area to share these *recipes* or whatever you call them. I've put an automatic translation option on all of the pages, since you say your group is global. If you're good with that, it's ready to test."

She says this so fast that my brain is racing to keep up. It sounds like the perfect platform to reunite the far-flung Flame-fingers and allow them to share their secrets.

"So would my group…" I pause and look around, but no one is close enough to overhear, "…be able to sign onto the same platform?"

"Yes, but for obvious security measures, seeing as you are two completely different entities, each with your own secrets, you will only share access to certain parts of the other group's database. Which parts those are will need to be decided by each group." She says all this with absolutely no expression, unless "bored stiff" counts as an expression, in which case she's nailing it.

"Okay, so what do you need now?" Siaka asks her.

"Guinea pigs," she says. "We need to beta test. Could you get together a group of FF volunteers—say, ten–preferably from different countries? Then we can test the translations and global login capabilities, to start with. We'll do any troubleshooting we need and be ready to launch in a couple of weeks."

"Should we do that with my group, too?" I ask her. I wondered if there was a code name for the bardia, seeing as she used "FF" for Flame-fingers.

"I don't see why not. We'll run the tests separately, for now, keeping the systems separate until you decide what data will be shared and what will remain private to your respective groups."

Okay, for a sixteen-year-old, this girl is scary-smart. I look at Siaka. "I'll explain it all to Gaspard so he can tell me what he wants to share."

"We'll ask Charlotte to give her input," Siaka says. "She's the one you'll be taking over bardia database management from."

"Great. Let's go," I say, ready to get out of there.

"I can come along and describe what Livia…"

She shoots him the rankest stink-eye imaginable.

"…*Liv* has set up so you guys can get started," Siaka says, and turns to go.

I start to say goodbye, but her eyes are already glued to her screen and her headphones back on.

"She's really a sweetheart under that impenetrable armor," Siaka says as we walk away.

"Adorable." I glance back. Her eyes not leaving her screen for a second, Liv raises her hand and, instead of waving goodbye, gives me the finger.

Chapter Eight

"Are you sure you guys are related?" I ask as Siaka and I step out into the sunshine. The burnouts have disappeared, leaving empty beer cans and a lingering smell of cannabis.

"What do you mean?" he asks, holding the gate open for me.

"I mean you're one of the most positive people I've met in a long time. She looks like her dog got run over and she's holding me personally responsible."

Siaka laughs. "Yeah, our moms are sisters, but we couldn't have been brought up more differently. She had a lot of pressure from her parents to achieve and decided to go her own way. My parents were just happy that helping my mom morphed into a passion for chemistry, which could result in an actual salary-paying job. Liv and I share genes but that's about it."

My cell phone buzzes in my pocket. Unknown number. Not odd, since Bran is the only contact I've ever had in this phone.

"Hey, Louis. It's Charlotte. Instead of coming home, want to meet somewhere?"

"Sure," I say, wondering what's up.

"Meet us at Abbesses," she says.

"Abbesses, the Métro stop?" I ask, and she confirms.

"I can take you," Siaka offers.

"Sure you don't mind?"

He smiles and hands me the helmet.

This time, I make sure there are no warm fuzzies going on between us during the ride. *Just a colleague. Just a colleague,* I repeat in my mind as the Vespa zips back in the direction we came from. Once in the cobblestone square next to Abbesses, Siaka parks the Vespa, while I look around. I know this place like the back of my hand. Nothing's changed.

The air is thick with the sweet aroma of candied peanuts. The merry-go-round next to the Métro entrance is lit up with green and red lights and tinny, old fashioned carnival music pipes out. I probably rode that carousel five hundred times between the age I could first sit up by myself and around nine, when I was finally too embarrassed.

Siaka catches me staring and looks amused. "Want to try it out? I have some change." He digs into his pocket.

I laugh. "No. But I used to ride this all the time when I was little."

"No way," he says. "This is your old hood?"

"Hey guys!" Charlotte waves as she walks toward us across the square. She's accompanied by a tall, pretty girl with short strawberry-blonde hair and freckles.

They lean in to give Siaka cheek kisses, then the tall girl turns to give me the *bises* too. "I'm Georgia," she says.

"You're Kate's sister!" I study her face for any resemblance but see none.

"And you're Louis…bad boy turned good. Or at least we hope you have. Kate thinks so, anyway."

"Arthur's here." Charlotte points to the air above our heads.

"I'm just here to make sure *he* behaves himself," Georgia says, winking. She has a southern accent that sounds straight out of *Gone With the Wind*. (Yes, believe it or not, I have seen that film. Bran has a penchant for old American movies, even though most of them are super politically incorrect.)

"This isn't an official out-looking-for-danger human-saving patrol," Charlotte explains, "or else Georgia wouldn't be along."

"Hey," Georgia says, looking offended.

Charlotte ignores her and continues, "So Siaka's welcome to join us. The game plan is to take you places you might have gone as a numa. See if anything jogs loose a memory that could be useful or see if there's renewed numa activity in the old places. I thought we'd start with your home."

"Even though your 'life' as a numa didn't start until Violette had you picked up at the morgue," Georgia adds.

We all stare at her. "What?" Georgia asks innocently. "I do my homework. Especially if it includes juicy gossip. And your story is a hundred percent pure juice, as far as I'm concerned."

"I'm…flattered?"

"Of course you are," Georgia says, winking. "I'm on your team by the way. Bardia Louis, all the way."

"There are teams?" I ask, feeling a twinge of panic.

"Don't pay attention to her," Charlotte says. She gives Georgia a mild look. "Hey, Arthur says he sees something shiny over there."

Georgia rolls her eyes. "Ha, ha. As if I could be so easily distracted." But she can't help glancing around and whispering, "Where?"

Let's go. I hear amusement in Arthur's volant voice.

As we amble north from the merry-go-round into the jumble of streets beyond, Charlotte says, "I know you've spoken to Kate about your past. But she's careful about guarding people's privacy, so I don't really know much. You feel like talking?"

I glance at Siaka and wonder what this information will do to his image of me. "You sure you want to hear? It's not pretty."

"We're dead," Charlotte replies. "None of us have pretty pasts."

"Except me," Georgia interjects. "I mean, the dead part. My past isn't that pretty either."

Bran had told me her story. She once dated Lucien, then the head of Paris's numa, and almost got everyone destroyed.

I spent centuries enabling a psychopath, Arthur adds.

Siaka remains silent, but grins. Well-acquainted with the group, he's enjoying the show.

"Point taken," I say. "Okay…well…my dad disappeared when I was nine. Mom did what she could to support me and my brother and sister, but when I was thirteen, she met a man named Frankie who promised to take care of us. As soon as he moved in, he quit his job and split his time between drinking beer on the couch and going out with his friends. He was a violent drunk. When he and Mom fought, she had me lock myself in the bedroom with my brother and sister." I feel my throat constricting and take a deep breath before continuing.

"One day, I came home early to check on my sister who had stayed home sick from school. There was a man in our bedroom, watching her sleep. It turned out Frankie made his beer money by selling drugs, and this was one of his clients. I told my mom, and she threatened to kick Frankie out. He responded by giving my brother a broken arm and my mom a black eye.

"I knew I couldn't fight him. So, I did the only thing I could think of to protect my family. When Frankie was passed out, I used his phone to call his drug supplier and told him Frankie had been skimming off the profits. Some guys were sent to confront him, and in the resulting fight, Frankie was killed. But so were my brother and I."

My story over, I glance at Siaka. He's concentrating on the cobblestones as our group heads up a narrow one-way street.

"You betrayed Frankie to his death," Charlotte says.

I nod. "A technicality, but it meant I would turn numa if I had revenant genes, or whatever. Violette was trying to build an army and was using Nicolas, her seer, to find newly-created numa. He spotted my aura and picked me up in the morgue."

Charlotte wraps an arm around my shoulder. "Well, I for one am glad that Kate saw the golden threads in your aura. You'll make a much better bardia than numa."

I smile. "Thanks."

"So, your sister and mother are still alive?" Siaka asks.

"Yes," I reply. "Gaspard had them moved for their safety. He gives me updates. Mom has a good job and my sister's in middle school." My throat squeezes tight the way it always does when I think of them. I won't ever get to see them again. But I'm glad they're safe.

Charlotte interrupts my thoughts. "Hey…isn't that it?"

We're standing in front of my old apartment building. *It's the first floor flat on the courtyard, right?* Arthur asks in my mind.

"Yes," I reply.

There's silence for a moment, and then he's back. There's a family living there. A man and woman with their baby.

I relay his report to the others, unable to avoid an empty feeling. Life in Paris has gone on. Without me.

Siaka places a hand on my shoulder. "You okay?"

I shrug.

"You should say goodbye."

I look at him quizzically, as do Charlotte and Georgia.

"My mother believed that buildings are alive," he explains. "This was your home, whatever good or bad things happened here. You should thank it and say goodbye. At least, that's what Mom would have done." He has a smile on his face like he's joking, but underneath, I glimpse something totally serious.

"What am I supposed to say?"

"Just ad lib it," he suggests.

"Um, okay." I turn toward the building, and give a weird little bow, not dissimilar to the one I gave Gaspard. "33, rue André del Sarte, thank you for housing my family. May your façade stay ungraffitied, and…may you never be torn down?" I turn to Siaka, who is now laughing.

Charlotte and Georgia give me a round of applause, and I bow again, this time deeply.

"Hey, if you can ad lib a Flame-finger house blessing, Bran definitely picked the right person for the job!" Georgia says, as we walk back to the Métro.

"Agreed," says Charlotte. "So…any memories of numa activities in your old neighborhood?"

I shook my head. "No. Further down toward Pigalle they had some bars. But most lived in the sixteenth arrondissement."

"Okay, let's check that out then," Charlotte said. "Next stop, sixteenth."

"I should actually get going. I'm having dinner with my dad," Siaka says. He stoops down to unchain the Vespa. "But I'll stop by La Maison tomorrow if that's okay. Louis and I need you to set him up on the bardia database."

"Sounds good," Charlotte says.

Siaka's gaze fixes on the air just to the right of my head, as if he spots something hovering there. "By the way, Arthur, Louis helped me prepare a new remedy for you to test when you reanimate."

That's right, I remember. Flame-fingers can see volant spirits.

Arthur replies to Siaka in my head. I hope it tastes better than the last one.

I translate, and Siaka laughs. "I'm not even telling you what was in the last one," he says to the air.

"You better not tell him what's in this one either," I say with a grin.

Joy, Arthur deadpans.

Siaka gives everyone cheek kisses, saving me for last. Despite my best efforts, his lips against my cheek turn my knees to Jell-O. He hops on his Vespa and drives away, all sexy leather-jacket biker guy. Once I tear my eyes from his receding form, I see Georgia grinning wickedly. "It's good to see you and Siaka get along so well, since you'll be spending a lot of time together."

My ears get hot and my face flushes. Charlotte is making a great effort not to laugh. "Shall we move on?" I suggest.

"*Or*...we could keep standing here watching you watch Siaka drive away," Georgia says, looking like the Cheshire Cat.

Don't listen to her, Arthur says. Georgia will 'ship' any two people whose eyes meet for more than a millisecond.

I clear my throat to hide my embarrassment. "We can go now," I say.

***

We spend the next couple of hours visiting places I went when I was a numa, starting with the luxury apartments where Nicolas and other important numa lived in the sixteenth arrondissement—the wealthy part of town.

By the time we get to Judas, the next stop on Charlotte's itinerary, it's pushing nine p.m. "So this is the place we fought those Numa Army guys a couple of days ago," she says.

"You already know the bar was owned by the numa," I say. "Violette came here a few times to meet with the human manager. Before that it was run by—"

"My old boyfriend. Yes, we all know," snaps Georgia, who's been silent since we neared the bar. "I was partying here when Lucien kidnapped me, took me to La Maison, and used me as bait to get to Vincent's dormant body. Do you guys mind if I hang back on this one?"

Her face has turned a sickly shade of green, as if she's going to be sick right there on the sidewalk. But as she turns to walk off, a huge, bearded guy with a motorcycle jacket, leather pants, and enough skull and crossbones jewelry to open a Halloween shop comes walking toward us.

"No way," Charlotte says, her hand drifting toward her waist. *She's carrying a sword*, I realize. It's hidden so well under her long vintage raincoat that I hadn't noticed it.

"It's him. Of course I'm sure," she says to the air. "What do you mean he doesn't recognize us?"

The guy barely glances at us as he strides by. Charlotte eases her hand from the hidden sword and gapes after him.

Georgia cops on to the fact that someone of interest is getting away, and calls after him, "Well, hey there, handsome."

The guy hesitates, then turns.

Georgia rests her hand on her hip. "Don't you remember me?" She saunters up to him, totally unafraid.

He looks her up and down. "Can't say that I do."

Georgia presses her hand to her chest like she's offended. "What? You were totally flirting with me the other night. Wasn't he, Elise?"

Charlotte strolls up and takes over for Georgia, who's winging it and obviously has no idea who the guy is.

"Surely you remember *me*," Charlotte says. "Remember, the sword fighting?"

He stares at her like she's crazy. "Sword fighting?"

"Sword fighting," Charlotte confirms. "You had this big-ass sword and were showing us your mad combat skills."

The guy frowns, like he thinks we're playing a joke on him. He glances at me and I shrug.

"I've never held a sword," he says. "I wouldn't even know what to do with one."

"Are you sure?" Charlotte asks. "It was a couple of nights ago. You had two friends with you, and the three of you were showing off like sword fighting maniacs."

At the mentions of his two "friends," the guy's face shuts down. "I don't know what you're talking about. I've never seen either of you before in my life." He says it likes he means it. He doesn't seem to be lying. He turns and walks away.

Back of his arm. The tattoo. Take a picture, Arthur says in my head.

I whip my phone out to get a clear photo. Georgia and Charlotte crowd around me as I zoom in and tap the shutter icon.

It's right there. The N.A. and broken swastika symbol. Whatever the *Numa Army* is, this guy's definitely part of it.

Chapter Nine

Ambrose greets us at the front door. "Finally!" he says. "Jeanne won't let us eat until everyone's here." He grabs me around the neck in a playful but all-too-realistic stranglehold. "So, how's your first day been, newbie? Good, huh? Work up an appetite? Let's get you some food. Then a workout."

"Maybe Louis would prefer getting moved into his room to a late-night workout," Charlotte says, gesturing at my bag, which still sits inside the front door.

Ambrose ignores her and pulls me toward the kitchen. "Do you realize that if you die now, each time, you'll transform back into this…" he waves his hand up and down as if displaying an underwhelming specimen, "…not quite peak form."

"I think Bran is hoping Louis *won't* die until he's a little older," Charlotte rebuts. "Which should give you plenty of time to play Louis's personal trainer…if he even wants you to!" She loops her arm through mine and accompanies us down the back hallway toward the kitchen.

Ambrose tips his head to the side, as though he's listening. He chuckles. "Arthur says I shouldn't assume everyone wants to be as jacked as me. Which is ridiculous. Of course they do! Let's call it a compromise. We won't let you die until you get at least as tall and as ripped as me. Then…" He makes a *squeech* kind of noise and draws his finger across his throat.

Charlotte leans in. "Don't let him push you around, Louis. He's under the impression that you're here solely for his entertainment."

Ambrose throws open the kitchen doors, and we walk in to see Jeanne pulling an enormous pan of lasagna from the oven. The undisputed house mom at La Maison, her gray hair is stacked up in a bun, and her plump figure and rosy cheeks make her look like she'd give the best hugs ever. Even so, I've decided to bide my time until she offers. Beside her, two bowls of salad sit on the counter and a tray of steaming garlic bread is cooling on a sideboard. My mouth starts watering like someone turned on a tap.

But when I tear my eyes away from the food, I completely forget about the meal. Because there, at the long dining table, Vincent—the same guy who served my ass to me on a plate at this morning's meeting—is serving apple sauce to a toddler sitting in a highchair.

I realize my mouth is hanging open but am unable to do anything about it.

Vincent sees me and frowns. "How'd it go?" he asks Charlotte.

"Let's get some food in front of us first," Ambrose interjects before she can answer, "then they can tell us everything." He carries over the tray of garlic bread and rips off a fist-sized piece to put on his plate.

I'm agog. Everyone's acting like it's a totally normal thing for the Head of France's revenants to be feeding a child in bardia headquarters, the same place from where we're planning an attack on the forces of evil.

The child stabs Vincent—scary Vincent—in the hand with her spoon to get his attention. Not only does it work, but he smiles and says how clever she is.

Mind. Officially. Blown.

From everything Bran taught me, revenants can't procreate. The three days a month we're dead pretty much guarantees that. Everything in our body stops during that time, which makes it impossible to host life. So, this can't be Vincent's child. Or anyone else here, except…

"Jeanne, is this your baby?" I ask, since she's the only human in the room. I immediately feel like an idiot because everyone turns and stares at me like…an idiot.

"My little Louis!" Jeanne squeals, setting the lasagna on a cooling rack and bustling over to give me the *bises*. "You are here! The last time I saw you, you had an arrow sticking out of your forehead. It was lodged in there so firmly that I couldn't pull it out and—"

"You had to call me to help," Ambrose finishes for her.

I try not to dwell on the mental image of an arrow sticking out of my skull.

Jeanne continues. "To answer your question, she is three, *cheri*, so she is not a baby. And, although I do have a granddaughter her age, she is not mine."

"Odette is ours," Kate says, walking out of the pantry with a bowl of strawberries. She plops it down in front of the baby…toddler…whatever…and says, "Vincent and I adopted her."

"Adopted?" I ask, stunned. *But who would adopt to a revenant?* Then, remembering that Kate can read my thoughts, I try to quash the idea before I offend her.

Kate gives Vincent a look that says, *Stop being so unfriendly and talk.*

Vincent scoots his seat back and wipes apple sauce off his hand. "It was a private adoption," he says, not quite looking at me, but at least talking. "I was engaged when I was human. Hélène, my fiancée, was murdered. This is the great-great-grandchild of her sister. I've been keeping an eye on the family over the years."

This is another thing I've learned about revenants—stalking the living is one of our driving forces, as well as a weakness. It made Charles to try to commit suicide by handing himself over to the numa.

"Odette's mother died in a car wreck, and there was no family left to take her," he continues.

"So you…?"

"Adopted her," Vincent says, looking at me like I'm slow-witted.

Kate picks up the conversation. "Meet the youngest member of La Maison—Odette Mercier-Delacroix. Gaspard can't wait to get a miniature sword into her hands, and Ambrose…well."

Ambrose is already crouched down next to the little girl and pulls faces to make her laugh. She pats apple sauce onto his forehead and says, "Bro-bros pwitty."

"Wow," is all I can think to say. I don't know why I'm so shocked. Maybe it's because I thought I was moving into a house of warriors, and this looks more like…a family. Something aches inside me.

Kate senses my discomfort. "Just let me know if La Maison is too stuffy for you, with a child here and all. You're welcome to choose one of the other group houses. The Mouzaïa house, for example, Genevieve's old house. I just thought you might want to start out here, where all the decisions are being made."

I shake my head. "Even if you had asked my opinion, La Maison would still be my first choice."

Charlotte grins. "We like you too."

Kate leans over to give me a supportive pat on the arm, and I notice the large sapphire on her ring finger. "Are you?" I begin.

She shoots a sideways glance at Vincent. He notices but turns back to pop a strawberry into Odette's mouth. "It's an engagement ring," she clarifies.

"Congratulations," I say.

"Yeah, we've been saying that too," Charlotte says, nudging Kate playfully, "for the last three years."

"We'll most likely live forever," Kate replies breezily. "I don't see why everyone's in such a rush." She turns to drape her arms around Vincent's neck. "I don't need a paper and a ceremony to prove my love for you."

"Maybe, but it wouldn't hurt," Vincent mumbles under his breath.

With perfect timing, Gaspard walks into the kitchen, distracting everyone from the uncomfortable conversation. Jeanne announces, "We're all here. *Bon appétit!*" before sweeping Odette into her arms and out the back door into the garden, "to play while the big people eat."

"Thank you!" Kate calls as the door swings shut behind them.

"So, what did you find?" Gaspard revenant asks once we're all settled and eating.

Charlotte speaks first. "Louis took us past several old numa locations."

"There wasn't much to see," I add. "We made a list of everyone I could remember living at each old address. When we spoke to a few of the building managers, it's definitely all new families living in the buildings. No signs of the old inhabitants."

Gaspard nods, like he expected that news. "I personally went through Jean-Baptiste's property lists after the Final Battle and made sure the apartments he had ceded to the numa were rented out to people wholly unrelated to their activities. It is good you checked things out in person."

"Things got weird, though, when we passed by Judas," Charlotte says. She turns to Ambrose. "One of those bouncers we fought the other night was there, and he didn't even remember me."

He freezes. "The big one with the beard?"

"They were all big with beards," she replies.

Gaspard wrinkles his nose. "It's so unkempt the way they grow them now, uncombed and untrimmed. Completely unsanitary. And they call it *hip*." He pronounces this last word like it is almost beneath him.

"Anyway," Charlotte says, "it wasn't the guy Ambrose and I had in our car. It was one of the others. Louis got a photo of his tattoo, and it's the same as his friend's."

I pull the photo up on my phone and pass it around. Gaspard looks at it for an extra-long moment. "Identical to the other. A three-armed swastika," he muses. "It's not balanced like a triskelion. It's like one arm has been broken off. What could the three mean? Three days that revenants are dead. Our Third Age, which dated from around 1800 C.E. until Kate ushered in the

Fourth Age with the Final Battle. Three types of magical beings. Bayati, revenants and Flame-fingers."

"Well, whatever it means, now we know that at least two of the guys have the tattoo, and they were all fighting us for no reason," Ambrose says.

"No reason besides a furious World War II hero getting all up in their faces," Charlotte points out.

"I didn't like the way they were looking at you," Ambrose insists.

"I could have handled them myself."

"And you did!" Ambrose agrees quickly. "You totally didn't even need me there."

They stare each other down for a couple of seconds before Charlotte cracks a smile. She gives his chin a squeeze. "You are getting so good at this, cupcake."

Ambrose looks relieved and, leaning over, whispers to me, "You're not supposed to 'protect' your wife, but when you step back and let them fight, they yell at you for not having their back."

"Sounds like you've got it figured out," I reply with a grin.

"If we dismiss the theory that they attacked because of Ambrose getting 'in their face,'" Gaspard says, pulling us back onto the subject, "one must wonder if it was because they recognized you. If the numa have humans working for them, they could easily be passing around photographs of the bardia. Telling their human henchmen to attack on sight."

Charlotte shakes her head. "Not today, at least. Arthur was volant and told me the guy didn't recognize me."

"Where *is* Arthur?" Kate asks, glancing around the kitchen.

"He said he was seeing Georgia home," I say.

Ambrose snorts, blowing breadcrumbs across the table. "So, they're back on. Ha! How long do you give it this time, Gaspard?"

Gaspard shakes his head. "Like I have said, Ambrose, I refuse to place money on people's romantic attachments."

"Okay. No money. But if this lasts a month, I'll sharpen every blade in the armory," Ambrose proposes.

"Fine. If it doesn't, I allow you to select our Friday Night Film until All Saints' week."

"Make it until Christmas, and you've a deal."

Gaspard huffs. "Fine, but I'm not watching anything with speeding automobiles and explosions. And no romances set in any era after the nineteenth century, comedic or not."

Ambrose smiles widely. "I can live with that."

"Do I hear bets being placed on my granddaughter's love life?" A striking older woman appears in the doorway. She's probably in her sixties and wears high heel shoes, an expensive-looking coral suit, perfectly set hair, and understated but expertly-applied makeup. She must be Georgia and Kate's grandmother. And, with a shock, I remember where I last saw her.

Clearly, she recognizes me as well, because she pauses, eying me. I push back my plate and rise to face her.

She lifts her chin. "The last time I saw you, you were holding a knife to my back. It's Louis, isn't it?"

I nod guiltily. I helped Violette hold Kate's grandmother hostage at the Crillon Hotel, as part of a plan to bait Vincent and Kate. It was not my finest hour.

"No one told me Louis would be coming," Mamie says to the room.

"It was only decided a couple of days ago," Kate replies. "And honestly, I had planned on having an informal get-together. I didn't know you were stopping by."

"Yes, well, I decided to pick up my great-granddaughter early," Mamie says, casting a look around the room. She glances back to me, and her face tightens. "I hear you've changed."

"I have." My chest aches with guilt and regret. I swallow down the lump in my throat. "But I'm truly sorry for the part I played."

The woman sniffs and holds her head a little bit higher. "Well, Kate has told me what you did for her when she…animated." She hesitates before saying that last word. Even after five years, she doesn't look comfortable with it. I don't blame her. Knowing your granddaughter is undead can't be easy to accept.

"Helping her escape that horrible Violette. I owe you my gratitude that she is here today. So, let's allow bygones be bygones. Is he…" She glances at the table, then forces her gaze back to me. "Are you going to be living here?"

"Yes, he is," Kate says. "And I would be happy to organize a time when the three of us can have a chat. I think, Mamie, that after hearing Louis's story, you will discover he's a very special case."

The older woman nods. Just then, Jeanne opens the back door and Odette runs across the room to her great-grandmother. Mamie throws her arms open wide. "Who's my darling little cabbage?"

I return to the table, relieved to have survived the encounter, but feeling shaken.

"Workout?" Ambrose offers, before scooping an enormous slice of tiramisu into his mouth.

"Nah," I say, picking up my plate and taking it to the counter. "I think I'll get moved in." Mamie's words made me feel like an alien in the house. Maybe getting my stuff moved in and having some time to myself will make me feel more at home.

Jeanne waves me away from the dishes. "I prepared Jules's room for you," she says. "It's the 'bachelor pad,' and he is most definitely no longer a bachelor. He and Ava visit so rarely from New York. Anyway, she would probably thank you for taking over the space he occupied during his wild years," she says with a wink. "Give me a minute, and I'll show you where it is."

"Don't worry," I say. "Just tell me, I can find it."

"Okay, but first…" She takes a pair of scissors from the counter, and in one swift motion takes a strand of my hair and snips it off. She carries the lock of hair to the counter and tucks it into a colorful enamel box the size of a teacup.

"Um, what was that for?" I ask, stunned.

Vincent gives a ghost of a smile. "Just call it life insurance," he says, making Kate laugh.

"Now," says Jeanne, wiping her hands on her apron, "up the grand staircase to the library, down the hall, and up another little flight of stairs. You can't miss it."

"Thanks," I say. "And thank you for the best meal I've had in…oh, a bit over five years."

"Bran's cooking is that bad?"

"Don't tell him I said so," I joke. But as I leave the kitchen's atmosphere of warm conviviality and head toward my new room, it doesn't matter that I'm in a house of people who, for the most part, accept me…who might even want me there. I still feel completely alone.

Chapter Ten

A battle axe slices so close to my ear that I want to check for blood. But there's no time: a spiked mace is approaching the other side of my head with frightening speed. I duck and fall to the right, taking the ground on one shoulder to roll across my back. I spring back to my feet in time to raise my sword just as the axe swings back down.

"Yes!" I yell, blocking Ambrose's weapon by its wooden hilt. Jerking it forward, I yank the axe from his grasp, and it crashes to the ground.

I win this round, but in case Ambrose rebounds with another attack, I skip back, out of his strike zone. I use the shoulder of my T-shirt to wipe away sweat that's dripping into my eyes.

A voice comes from the stairs above us. "Ambrose, you might consider lightening up. Louis's going to change his mind and move back to Brittany." Kate perches on the edge of a step. Then I see who's next to her, and my mouth feels dry as sand.

"Hi," I manage to croak.

Siaka slow claps. My guts are in a knot, but his smile lights a flame inside my chest. "You're actually keeping up with Ambrose," he calls. "I'm impressed!"

I allow myself a quick glance at the mirror. Normally tan, I'm now bright red. I look like someone just fished an underweight lobster out of the sea and shoved a sword into its claws. Beside me, Ambrose is pumped like a superhero, his ebony skin barely damp with sweat.

"That might have just been the hardest workout I have ever had," I say, gasping for breath. "Can we call it a day?"

"If you agree to a rematch tomorrow, same time, same place," he says, doing a fancy baton spin with the battle axe. He tosses it toward the pegs on the wall, and it actually lands right side up and settles into place. Everything this guy does is impressive. To say he's intimidating would be the understatement of the century. He drapes a towel around his shoulders and heads toward the showers.

"I'm just delivering Siaka," Kate says, rising to her feet, "instead of hanging out with you guys, which would be more fun. Got a meeting in the library." She rolls her eyes dramatically and disappears up the stairs.

"Bran and I came over together," Siaka says. "He's working with Kate and Vincent today. I thought you and I could go to the lab."

"Sure," I say, leaning forward, hands on knees, trying to catch my breath. My hair is dripping with sweat. "Do I have time for a shower?"

"Um… that's probably a good idea," he says. "Not that I'm close enough to smell. Just guessing."

I jokingly sniff my underarm. Ugh, acrid. "You guessed right. Shower's imperative. I'll be up in a few."

Siaka turns to follow Kate up the stairs, and I turn to see Ambrose's head above one of the shower cubicles, emerging from a cloud of steam. He looks at me and laughs. "I didn't know it was humanly possible to sweat as much as you do."

"At least I can beat you at something," I say.

"Don't worry, shrimp," he says, disappearing under the spray. "I'll get you jacked in no time. But if you think you'll ever beat me, you just keep on dreaming."

***

The basement lab at Le Corbeau feels different today. No Bran to be the intermediary. No bustling around with a group activity. Just Siaka and me. The room feels charged with an airborne electrical current that zaps me every time he gets close. He obviously doesn't feel it, acting as friendly and natural as the day before, whereas I'm stiff, conscious of every word I say.

I can't let him know how he affects me, or it will ruin everything. It'll make things awkward at the very least, and my new kindred have entrusted me with this important role. I'll be damned if I mess it up just because of a crush.

"Are you always so distracted after a workout?" Siaka asks as he grabs a stack of notebooks off a counter. Wedging them under his arm, he fishes for a set of keys in his jacket pocket.

"What do you mean?" I ask, immediately self-conscious.

"You're so quiet."

"Sorry, just, well…I'm used to being by myself most of the time. Or with Bran, which is practically the same."

Laughing, he sticks a key in a door at the end of the lab and turns the knob. Switching on the light, he holds the door open for me, and I walk into an office furnished with two desks, a clutter of unmatching chairs, and shelves crammed full of books and papers. On the bigger, more modern desk sits a large, expensive-looking monitor and under it what looks like the latest, most powerful computer tower.

The smaller desk is an antique and holds a lamp, a stack of notebooks, and an ancient silver chalice crammed with a dozen or so sharpened pencils. A chunky black dial telephone and a bound book with *Addresses* printed on the cover make it look like the whole thing was teleported, accessories intact, from the 1950s.

"I think I can guess whose desk is whose."

Siaka smiles widely, concentrating on typing something into his phone. In seconds, rap music is playing through a speaker system mounted near the ceiling.

"I've been pushing and shoving my uncle towards the twenty-first century, and he's fought me the whole way," he says. "He claims his system works for him and my system works for me, so we're leaving it at that."

I laugh. "That's pretty much the same thing he said to me, word for word. But he was happy to set up an office for me in his house in Brittany and stock it with all the equipment I asked for."

"Same here," Siaka says, flopping down into his ergonomic chair and switching on the computer. He angles his monitor toward me. "Grab a chair. There's enough room for both of us on my desk," he says. "Did you bring Charlotte's laptop?"

I pull a chair up next to his, trying to ignore the fact that there are only about eight inches separating his arm from mine. If the butterflies in my stomach would chill out, I might be able to concentrate. "Um…no, this is the 'house' laptop. The one they use for communicating with the Worldwide Consortium. I guess it's mine now."

Siaka swings around to face me, his expression serious. "Dude, are you okay?" he asks. He's so close now that I can see his jade eyes are flecked with gold around the pupil. It would be so easy to lean forward, tilt my head, and… My eyes dart to his lips, my heart stutters fast and hard, and I can't breathe. It feels like time stretches on for minutes, but I know it's only been a second, as I use all of my willpower to break the magnetic pull between us and turn away.

Pretending that my insides haven't just been ripped out of my body, reassembled, and shoved back in, I lean over, unzip the computer bag, pull the laptop out and plonk it on the desk. Then, running my hands through my hair, I tuck it behind my ears, and feel marginally more composed.

"Seriously," Siaka prods. "What's up?"

I don't look at him this time. I don't dare. "Like I said, I haven't had much practice at being sociable for a really long time. I'm not used to talking to people in real life." I force myself to chuckle as I open the laptop and type in the password Charlotte gave me. "It might take a while to transition out of hermit mode."

My computer's desktop opens to show a row of icons glowing against a background photo of…

"Oh. My. God," Siaka breathes, looking over my shoulder at the screen.

It's Ambrose, wearing his World War II army cap, a pair of worn jeans, his thick gold wedding band, and…nothing else but burnished ebony skin. Muscles bulging, twelve-pack sculpted, and a smoldering look in his eyes that would hands-down land him Mr. January in one of those Hot Guy calendars. Across the bottom of the screen Charlotte has labeled the photo in big flowery letters, "My cupcake."

Siaka and I tear our eyes away from the screen, look at each other, and start laughing hysterically, wiping tears from our eyes.

"Okay, your first task is to replace Charlotte's desktop image, or neither of us are going to get any work done," Siaka says when he's able to talk again.

Thanks to the comic relief, I feel myself relaxing as I connect to the Wi-Fi and search the internet for a surfing image to replace Captain Cupcake. The music has settled into the perfect background beat as Siaka and I type into our computers. He disappears for a second and comes back with two ice cold cans of Coke. And suddenly, everything's fine. It feels natural to be here with this—yes, hot, but I can manage it now—guy, working side by side.

I pull up the bardia's database, and he logs into the temporary system he's been using to keep track of the Flame-fingers, and we compare data fields—names, addresses, emails—noting their order and making adjustments so the two systems are aligned.

"I took genealogy software and adapted it," he explains, showing me his screen, "so that each Flame-finger can indicate their 'lineage' and the origin of the information they're sharing."

He shows me a screen with a world map and clicks on France. Up pops a headshot of Bran, with the words underneath, "Bran Tandôrn, France, Flame-finger 2011-current." Siaka clicks on Bran's photo, and a family tree-style flowchart pops up. The image directly above Bran is a woman with wild curly blond hair and the name "Gwenhaël Tandôrn, France, Flame-finger 1977-2011." Above her is a black and white photo of a man who was obviously her father, and whose Flame-finger end date was 1977. Above him is an image of a woman that looked like it was scanned from one of those antique tintype photographs. Each person above her is simply identified by a name. They must have lived pre-photography.

"So, each *guérriseur* has their own page," Siaka says, and clicks on the image of Bran's mother. A profile page pops up with her photo in the upper left corner. The rest of the page is filled with information and links. "These links are to 'cures' or remedies that she either created herself or adapted and used." He clicks one of them, and a page comes up entitled, "Remedy for migraines in women of child-bearing age." There's a scan of a handwritten page in a journal, and then the text typed out underneath. At the bottom of the 'remedy' is a link to another Flame-finger's name, along with the word, 'origin.'

"Bran and I started with his family's journals that his mother passed on to him," Siaka says. "I've been typing them one by one into the database. There are a lot of them, and even more in our archives." He looks up at me. "Man, I wish I could take you there. It's this secret underground location next to the Cluny Museum. But revenants can't enter." He shakes his head like it's a shame, and although my curiosity is piqued, it's superseded by the notion that he would even want to take me there.

He looks back to the monitor and continues. "At the same time, Flame-fingers from around the world have begun sending us their lineage and their own 'family remedies.' I've been entering it all as it comes in. I flag the ones that look the most promising, especially those used to treat revenants. In the meantime, Bran and I try to duplicate the remedies in our lab."

He clicks on another page titled 'Testing Platform.' It's a table, with columns labeled Treatment Goal, Treatment Origin, Formulation, Comments, Bardia Testee and Results.

"Okay, here's where you come in," he says, and clicks on the first, Treatment Goal.

"Resisting Death," I read out loud. Under it are listed four treatments, each linked to the Flame-finger who submitted them. The first one reads, *Treatment: 'Eternal Tears' Origin: Amesbury, 17th century manuscript.* The Formulation field has yesterday's date and links to Bran's and Siaka's profile pages, since they were the Flame-fingers who reproduced the formula. Under the comments, Siaka types, "All original conditions respected." And he tabs over to "Bardia Testee" and types, "Arthur Poincaré."

"So, once Livia gets us connected with the new platform," Siaka says, "you'll be able to take over from here. Arthur will take the remedy and you will keep notes on how he responds and type it into the system. If there aren't any horrible side effects, we will greenlight it for other Flame-fingers to produce and bardia to test it across the world."

"Horrible side effects?" I ask. "Like what?"

"Well, the last one made Arthur's hair fall out," Siaka says with a grin. "It came back after his next dormancy. But for the entire month, he wouldn't leave La Maison without a ski cap, and he locked himself in his room whenever Georgia came over."

I turn back to my screen, where I've opened up the bardia's Worldwide Consortium database. A world map is lit with green circles, numbers popping up when you scroll over each one. A number at the bottom of the page calculates the international population of bardia at over ten thousand.

"This is going to be a massive project," I say.

"Yeah." Siaka sips his Coke and looks thoughtful. "But it's a fascinating subject. And there's the knowledge that if we find something that makes the bardia stronger, our work can help humanity.

"To be honest, now that you're here, I'm really looking forward to this. Just think. We've literally years of working on this…together!" He reaches out and pats me on the shoulder. It's one hundred percent Just Friendly, but I wasn't prepared, and the hairs on my arms stand on end. I scoot back in my chair and look away.

Okay, this isn't the Flame-finger energy pulse. Or not just. This is Big Feelings. As in my feelings for Siaka. How in the world am I going to handle working with this guy I'm so attracted to for years…even decades?

Siaka pulls his hand back. "I mean, only if you want to, of course." There's a seed of hurt in his voice. "Bran said you'd be up for it, but seriously, if you don't like the work, or don't…" He gets this look like something's dawning on him. "Or if you don't like your work *partner*, then I'm sure he can find someone else."

"Oh my god, no, it's not that," I sputter. "No, I totally dig this work. And you. And…" Oh no, now I'm babbling like an idiot. I try to come up with something that makes it sound like it's not personal. But it totally is.

"It's only that I thought I was coming to Paris to work with other bardia. Working with a Flame-finger is just…I wasn't expecting it," I say, trying to calm the panic in my voice.

"Oh," Siaka says. He looks at me strangely, like he's trying to decipher the text of one of his ancient recipes. And then his face contorts. "Oh. Okay, I get it. We Flame-fingers are just humans who happen to have gifts. We're not actually supernatural like you. So, you don't consider us equals."

"Oh my god, that's not at all what I meant," I say, starting to freak out. "Bran has been amazing. He healed me. I owe him so much. I love Flame-fingers. Seriously." I force myself to shut up before I say something even more stupid. But it doesn't matter, because Siaka's face has already slammed shut.

He swivels around in his chair to face his screen and starts furiously typing into the database. I watch him and wonder how in the world I'm going to survive working with him, without having a total breakdown.

Chapter Eleven

It's been an hour of pure, uninterrupted silence. A good helping of anguish served atop a burnt toast smell from the lab has me feeling green at the gills. Siaka and I sit a foot apart, typing into our computers and pretending a diplomatic disaster didn't just occur.

So when the door flies open, we both jump a foot out of our chairs. I grab my chest, like I'm having a heart attack and Siaka screams, "What the fuck?"

In the doorway stands a short, slight figure, chunky headphones over a purple knit cap over long black braids. Holey grey hoodie over a T-shirt and black jeans. All this layering topped by a smirk like she doesn't want to ruin her cool by laughing, but the sight of two guys scared witless is clearly too hilarious for her to maintain the deadpan.

"Yo," Liv says.

"Yo?" Siaka repeats incredulously. "You barge into my private lab space without warning? How did you even get in the front door? It's locked! Wait, no, I don't care. And you dare bust in all, 'Yo?' like you didn't just give us both a stroke?"

"Wassup?" she tries, then dumps a load of bags. Turning one upside down, she empties it unceremoniously onto Bran's desk. A river of candy, gum and cans of energy drinks spills out. She opens a large-screen laptop with a couple of external drives and a handful of USB hubs. All the while completely ignoring us.

Siaka stands, arms folded across his chest. "Cuz? Did you hear me? I did not know you were coming. I did not invite you. You don't just come barging into my personal space—"

"Like you did the other day?" she replies, concentrating on plugging a half-dozen devices into her computer, and then running the cords down under Siaka's desk. She stops when she gets to my legs, and stares up, waiting.

"Yeah, I'll just scoot back to let you by," I say.

She crawls past me under the desk to link the cords to Siaka's computer tower. Her task finished, she flops into Bran's chair, opens a bag of jelly Smurfs and starts typing madly into her keyboard. She's listening to Rage Against the Machine. It's so loud, I can hear the lyrics though her earphones.

Siaka shakes his head. "Sorry about that. She's not usually this... No, I take that back. She's always like this." He glances at her pile of candy, then at me. "It's actually lunch time. Should we go out and get something?"

So, one, he's talking to me again. And, two, I would love to get away from this sullen girl with a chip on her shoulder. But Charlotte told me to guard the bardia's computer with my life. "Technically, you're not even supposed to let Siaka use it," she'd told me.

"Um, I probably shouldn't leave..." I was about to say, 'my laptop,' but Siaka sighs and cuts me off.

"That's okay. I don't mind going for the two of us. Ham and cheese sandwich?"

I can tell from his face that he's still thinking I'm some kind of bardia bigot, but I don't know what to say that will clear up my mess, especially with his cousin sitting here looking like Billie Eilish's angry little sister. I settle for, "Yeah. That'd be great. Thanks."

He leaves, and now it's just me and Liv. Continuing to ignore me, she fiddles with another cord, plugging one end into her hub and draping the other behind the back of my desk. She pulls her headphones down around her neck and asks, "Do you mind?"

She doesn't look like she's about to dive under the desk again, so I'm not sure what she wants me to do.

"Mind?" I venture.

"Plug it into one of the USBs in the back of Siaka's tower." She has this uncanny ability to speak without showing any hint of emotion. Like, none.

I obey and duck under the desk. When I come back up, she's typing again on her keyboard, but has left her headphones down.

"Smurf?" she asks and nudges the candy bag a millimeter in my direction.

The last thing I want to put in my mouth is blue gelatin, but I'm so afraid of pissing her off that I pluck one from the bag. I chew quickly and swallow before I can taste it.

Liv's earphones are still around her neck, so I take that as an invitation. I mean, this has to be hacker code for, *Now you may speak to me.*

"So, Livia," I begin.

"Liv," she says, still staring at her screen.

"Oh yeah, sorry. Siaka always calls you Livia, so I—"

"Just Liv." This time she glances over at me and the right corner of her lip might be quirking up just a fraction of an inch. Or maybe not. It's too hard to call. In any case, she says, "Thanks."

Now we're getting somewhere, I think. Encouraged, I say, "I'm Louis."

"Yeah, I remember." Liv shoves another Smurf in her mouth and chases it with a gulp of Red Bull. The way her fingers race over the keyboard, it's like she's a part of the machine. Her hands pause, and she asks, "How many?"

"How many what?"

"How many of your kind? Or as you put it before, your 'group.'"

"Well…" I hesitate, unsure of how much she's supposed to know. Gaspard and Bran made it clear that I was working with Siaka. They didn't say anything about his cousin. Although, I suppose that since Siaka's mother was a Flame-finger, and she was Liv's aunt, Liv knows a lot already.

"It's not a trick question," Liv says, as though she's reading my mind. She turns her computer screen so that I can see the display. Her cursor blinks next to a data box that reads, 'Total # Users Group B.' I can see she has already filled in the 'Total # Users Group A' box with the number 187.

"There are only one hundred and eighty-seven Flame-fingers in the world?" I ask. That doesn't seem like a lot.

"Well, only one member of each *guérriseur* family is counted as having the gift. Bran and Siaka are the only Flame-fingers in France…that we know of. And outside of France, Bran's been able to track down a hundred and eighty-five. There's probably a lot more. They didn't really stay in touch over the years."

Liv has said more words in the last minute than she has the whole time I've known her. "You know a lot about the Flame-fingers."

She looks up from the monitor. "My family has been Flame-fingers ever since we can remember. My mother's actually the oldest daughter, so my grandmother should have given it to her. But Mom didn't want it, and her sister, Siaka's mom, did. That's why he has the gift now, and not me. So yes, I know a lot about Flame-fingers. It's my history. It's my birthright." She rolls her eyes. "Like I care."

Something tells me the nonchalance is an act. She *does* care. No wonder she has so much attitude with Siaka.

"Does Siaka know how you feel?" I ask.

"We've talked about it. I mean, it's kind of a moot point. Look at me. Can you imagine me as a *guérriseur*? I'd rather hack someone than heal them, any day." Her lips do that tiniest of upturns once again, which I suspect is the closest she ever gets to a smile. "So how many bardia?" She moves her curser on the database.

I peer at my screen, click into the homepage, and say, "It looks like there are around five thousand listed worldwide. The number varies depending on which listing I'm in. I haven't had time to figure it all out."

"Close enough," she says, typing again. "And in France?"

I click through on the map. "Around forty-five in Paris, and a couple hundred in the rest of the country. Again, that's approximate."

She enters the information, and then switches over to a blank page on her screen with lines of raw code. She starts typing into the middle of it. I look back at my laptop and read through the database pages one by one, trying to familiarize myself. But I'm too distracted to really let it sink in. All I can think about is that the girl sitting next to me is a veritable font of information about the boy I'm crushing on.

"So, what's Siaka like?" I hear the words tumble from my mouth before I can stop them and sit there, horrified. Liv taps a button on the headphones around her neck, and the screech of unintelligible music stops.

She studies my face. "What's Siaka like? As in…what *is* he like? Or what *does* he like?"

I squeeze my eyes shut and press them with the palms of my hands, trying—for just a split second—to erase the situation I just caused for myself. Hoping against hope that when I open my eyes Liv will have gone back to looking at her screen. But no, there she is, watching me.

"What *is* he like? Well, I'm his cousin, so one of my earliest memories is of him convincing me to eat sand out of the sandbox at Place des Vosges. I'm probably not the best person to vouch for his character.

"As for what he *likes*, well…his last girlfriend wasn't exactly what I would call a rocket scientist. Pretty, but dumb as a rock. I hope that answers your question."

She must see something in my face. A flash of despair, a shadow of disappointment, because as she switches her music on and fits the headphones back over her cap, she says, "But his last boyfriend…well, he wasn't bad."

Chapter Twelve

Soon after Siaka returns with our lunch, Liv packs up and goes, leaving an explosion of candy wrappers and sugar residue strewn across Bran's desk. I shovel it into a trash can, then scoot my stuff over. It seems awkward now to share a desk with my Flame-finger counterpart.

It must have been the wrong thing to do, because Siaka gets this look like something smells rotten and cranks the music. I can't do anything right with this guy. What's wrong with me?

We eat our sandwiches while working. The four feet between us is so charged with negativity I can practically see the sparks out the side of my eye. When I dare glance over, I see that Siaka is typing out some old Flame-finger text handwritten on a crumbling notebook. I click through the bardia's database, cleaning up files with incomplete or misspelled addresses and making a list of those lacking email addresses. I've got a lot of admin work to do before we can get up and running. And although it seems important, no one's talked about a deadline, so I'm guessing the schedule is ASAP.

Siaka's phone buzzes, and he tilts it forward to read a text. "Welp. We better go," he says. "Arthur's waking up from his dormancy."

I look at him quizzically.

"Bran and I decided the best time to test the remedies is just after a bardia has reanimated from their three-day dormancy." He shoots me a tense glance. "After *you've* reanimated."

"It's okay," I say, trying to make up for my previous blunder. "I'm not really one of them yet, so that's probably confusing for you." Oh shit. I know it's a disaster as soon as it comes out of my mouth.

Siaka looks at me like my words were a slap.

I scramble to fix things. "I don't mean confusing for you *personally*. I mean confusing for anyone. Because you're obviously really knowledgeable..." I trail off, feeling each word dig me in even deeper. As if that's possible.

Avoiding eye contact, we pack our stuff, leave the basement, and make our way through the shop. Siaka locks the door behind us and halfheartedly asks, "Scooter?"

"Sure," I reply. I hate the tension between us, but I don't dare try to talk it out for fear of saying something that ruins things for good. Because *if* I said what I truly feel—I mean, face it, the horrifying awkwardness is because I have a massive crush on him—well, I might as well turn in my resignation to Bran and Gaspard and tell them to find me a replacement.

I tuck my hair behind my ears, pull on the helmet Siaka hands me, and sit behind him on the scooter. Despite my best efforts to ignore it, I still feel his magnetic pull, and it takes all my resolve to resist wrapping myself around him. But gone is the sparkling feeling floating in the air. Instead, I smell exhaust each time we pass a car, and the glittering magic of Paris has morphed into a thick fog of suck.

I feel like taking the next train out of the city, but where would I even go? The place I lived the last five years isn't my home anymore. What am I going to do? Show up on my mom's doorstep and say, "Hey, Mom, I came back to life!" No, Paris is my home now. I have to make this work.

When we pull into the courtyard at La Maison, Bran is sitting on the edge of this angel fountain that always reminds me of Kate and Vincent. My mentor is chatting with Vincent, who holds Odette on his lap. She's wearing Bran's glasses, and her eyes are magnified to the size of eggs as she watches us climb off the scooter. She points as we walk toward them.

"Big," she says. Then taking the glasses off… "Little." Then back on. "Big!" And off. "Little!"

It's super-cute.

"Give the glasses back to Bran, Odette," Vincent says. "We wouldn't want him to hurt himself running into things."

Bran rolls his eyes comically. Odette giggles and says, "Don't hurt yourself, Bran."

I have this pang in my heart because I want to be a part of this, but I feel I'll have to earn it. My hunch is confirmed when Vincent glances up and gives me a polite nod instead of a smile.

Now that we're outside, in daylight, I see that Odette has large green eyes and strawberry blond hair. It's pulled up into two short ponytails on either side of her head, which is how my sister wore her hair at the same age. The pang in my heart flares and I look away.

"Hi, Siaka," says Odette, solemnly lifting her face to let him kiss her cheeks, left then right. She looks at me. "You live upstairs now. I tried to go in your room, but Mommy said no."

"I'm Louis," I say and lean over so that she can plant soggy kisses on my cheeks.

"You are kindred," she announces. "Bran and Siaka are *kind* of kindred. They are our most special friends. But if you live in our house, that means you are kindred. Right, Daddy?"

Vincent looks uncomfortable and tries to distract her by fixing one of her ponytails, but she won't let the subject drop. "Right, Daddy? Louis is kindred."

I try to let Vincent off the hook, and ask Bran, "Should we go check on Arthur?"

He stands and slips his glasses back on. "Yes. I was out here waiting for you when I was joined by such pleasant company." He ruffles Odette's hair, but she's digging in for the win with her father and pays him no attention.

As we walk toward the front door, I hear her say, "BroBrose says if someone lives in La Maison they're kindred, and BroBrose is always right. He told me that."

Bran chuckles as we pass through the front door. "Looks like you have a powerful ally, Louis. Vincent doesn't stand a chance when Odette makes up her mind about something."

"She's really something," I agree.

"She's more than you think," Bran says. I look at him quizzically. "I've told Vincent and Kate already, but I imagine they kept it to themselves. Odette has a role to play. An important one. But it will come later. That's all I know."

"But how?" I ask.

"Her aura." And that's the end of that. I'm getting used to Bran spouting mysterious prophecies, but with this one, I wish I had some spoilers.

We enter the house, pass the foyer and a sitting room, then through a series of doors. Bran leads the way, with Siaka standing stiffly aside to let me through first.

"Go ahead," I offer, but he shakes his head and waits for me. Things could not be more awkward. I give up. Once we're in Arthur's room, I try to forget about my failure with Siaka and watch Bran.

Arthur sits reading, propped up against a pillow in a four-poster bed that looks straight out of the Palace of Versailles. Next to the bed, on an equally ornate bedside table is an untouched tray of fruits and nuts along with bottles of water and juice.

"Finally, you're here," he says, putting his book down. I glance at the title. It's a self-help book about relationships. I try not to grin.

"I'm starving," Arthur tells me. "Bran forbade me from eating until you arrived."

"From what I can ascertain," Bran pipes up, "a remedy or cure is most effective if administered when the body is empty of liquids and food. Therefore, the optimal timing is just as a bardia reanimates."

"Being the bardia in question," Arthur says, "what kind of remedy have you got for me this time?"

Bran pulls a flacon from his pocket, uncorks it and hands it to Arthur. "I won't tell you what's in it," he says, "but it's meant to do the same thing the last four have: ease your craving for death so you're in full control of when you choose to die next."

Bran hands me a leather-bound journal and a pen. "Since you will be living under the same roof, you can record Arthur's reactions. Please write down anything relevant, then ask him the questions written inside the front cover."

"Okay." I pull up a chair and prop the journal on my knee. I glance at the last entry and write the date, time and Arthur's name in the same order.

"Go ahead," Bran says to Arthur. "Drink it."

Siaka pours a glass of water and waits. Arthur tips his head back, empties the flacon into his mouth, swallows, then—his face twisting into a grimace—grabs for the glass of water. Chugging it, he looks at us, eyes watering.

"First question," Bran prompts.

"Ah, Question 1. What did it taste like?" I read.

"Cat pee," Arthur responds.

I look up to see if he is joking. He's not. I jot down, "Taste: cat piss."

"Question 2," I continue. "Do you sense any aftertaste?"

"If possible, an even stronger note of cat piss, followed by what I would imagine floor polish tastes like." Arthur's nostrils are flaring, and it looks like he's trying not to throw up.

I write down his response, then run through the rest of the questions, noting no immediate physical reactions, no lightheadedness or swimming of vision. I get to the end of the list.

Satisfied, Bran stands and says, "Good, good. Louis will stay with you for the next hour to note any other immediate reactions."

"May I eat?" Arthur eyes the tray of food.

"Yes, of course," Bran replies.

Plucking up a date, he pops it in his mouth. "Mmmph," he moans, closing his eyes in ecstasy. "Oh my god, the first thing you eat after dormancy is always the best thing you've ever tasted."

Brans smiles and pats Arthur's shoulder. He turns to leave. "Siaka, there's a manuscript in the library that Gaspard thought you and I should have a look at."

"Let's go," Siaka agrees. And without giving me so much as a glance, he follows his uncle out of the room.

Chapter Thirteen

"Why don't you make yourself comfortable if you're going to be babysitting me?" Arthur suggests. He nods toward an overstuffed armchair across the room. I drag it near the bed and try to sit in a way that I can hold the notebook on my knee while trying to still look somewhat competent—I want to nail my very first job in La Maison. But the chair's so deep and cushy that I finally give up and scoot back, fold up my legs, and let it envelop me.

Arthur eats a few more things from the tray, then leans back and closes his eyes. I read in the notebook's previous entries that Bran and Siaka have tried four variations of potions on Arthur over the last few years. Side effects have ranged from temporary blindness (only temporary because the next time Arthur was dormant, his body reset and reanimated with sight intact) to the humiliating hair loss Bran mentioned. From the dates, it looks like Bran spaces out treatments by at least six months. Probably to measure long term effects—whether negative or positive.

I flip through to some sections further back listing non-medicinal treatments they've tried. Acupuncture, meditation, aromatherapy… "Thermal baths?" I ask incredulously.

Arthur opens his eyes, sees what I'm reading, and smiles. "Yeah, that was one of my favorites. Gaspard arranged a one-month stay in Ischia." Noting my lack of recognition, he explains. "It's a volcanic island off the coast of Italy. Famous for the healing hot springs on its beaches."

"Wow. That must have been really difficult for you," I say with mock pity.

"Yeah, even more difficult because I convinced my girlfriend—I mean, Georgia—to come with me." He grins slyly.

"Definitely better than cat-piss flavored potion," I agree. "So, are you not supposed to use the label 'girlfriend'?"

Arthur leans his head back, as if the mere subject exhausts him, but his grin remains. "Georgia is Georgia. She isn't *my girlfriend* because she isn't *anyone's anything*, as she likes to put it."

"But, from what Siaka says, you're doing all these…" I gesture to the notebook, "…experiments for her."

"That is true." Arthur's smile dissipates. "But then, I would do anything for her." No more joking around. Now he's one hundred percent earnest.

"Let me get this right." I lean forward out of my chair-cocoon. "You're how old?"

"I was born in 1472."

"So, you're over five hundred," I say. "I thought the desire to die grows less over the years. That bardia like you…"

"Us geriatrics?"

I laugh. "Yeah. That you can hold out for a really long time before feeling the urge to die saving someone."

"That's true. We can hold out," he replies. "I could age along with Georgia until I was around fifty. Sixty maybe. But after that, it would be like she was living with a drug addict. I've done it before. Let's just say I'm not the most pleasant person to be around after a thirty-year stretch." Looking tired, he closes his eyes, inhales deeply, then continues.

"So, let's say Georgia and I make it to fifty. Okay, she would be fifty-three and I would be fifty. I died a few months ago—accident—so she's technically three years older than me."

"Does that bother her?" I ask.

"*Au contraire.* She loves it. Calls herself a cougar," he says, wryly. "But if we both make it to fifty, she'll be at the prime of life. And I'll be bad tempered and shaky and itching to dive in front of every jaywalking pedestrian in hopes of getting run over by a delivery van."

He opens his eyes, pours himself a glass of water and takes a sip. "Already I can't offer her children, which she claims she doesn't want anyway. Then, there's the fact that I'm an integral part of an insular group of supernatural beings whose entire existence is dedicated to a cause. But she insists she's a part of the group too, since her sister is the Champion. I just feel like if I can get this one thing sorted out, maybe she will have me."

"Because she won't have you now?"

"At twenty-three, who knows what they want?" he replies. "She'll move here with me for a few days, then goes running back to her apartment in Batignolles saying she needs space. Or I'll stay there with her, and after a couple weeks when I offer to help pay for utilities or something, she freaks out and says, 'What do you think we are, grown-ups?'"

"Wait. Doesn't she have to be a grown-up to pay her bills?"

"She put everything on automatic payment. And she has this online assistant who takes care of all the other 'boring details' of her life."

"She has an assistant?" I'm not sure why this is so surprising to me.

"Georgia runs her own extremely successful event planning business," Arthur replies, proudly. Which seems kind of messed up. He's been saving lives for five centuries and she throws parties. Shouldn't she be the one who's proud to be with him?

Noticing my expression, he laughs. "I know. Event planning sounds frivolous, right? Like non-stop parties. That *is* how it started. Georgia's always been the consummate party girl, so it was a natural extension of her personality. But get this…."

He leans toward me, eyes bright with excitement. "For every ten launch parties, corporate functions, or celebrity mixers she organizes, she hosts a charity benefit. She'll get Adidas to sponsor a dance party for underprivileged teens, where every kid goes home with a pair of top-of-the-line shoes. Or get Red Bull to pay for ski camp for inner-city kids whose families normally wouldn't be able to send them to the Alps. Believe me, Louis. This girl is one of a kind."

When he talks about Georgia, Arthur's face is transfigured. His handsome features radiate joy. And I feel that pang again. The pang of craving. Of desire. Not just the desire to fit in—to have a group who accepts and values me. But to have my own person to love. Someone I can feel for like Arthur feels about Georgia.

He interrupts my musing with his own question. "So, I'm barely back to life here, but I couldn't help notice some…frostiness between you and Siaka."

Wow. Is it that obvious? "Um, yeah, I guess five years in Brittany was enough time to lose all my social skills. It might take me a while to get used to being around people," I say.

"Is that it?" Arthur asks. "You seemed to get on extremely well yesterday. Maybe well enough to cause a conflict of interest?"

Oh my god. Georgia has definitely talked to him about what she saw between me and Siaka. Or, rather, me toward Siaka. "Um, that's not… It's not!" I sputter. "I mean, you guys brought me here to do a job. And that's totally what I'm going to do. 'Conflict of interest' can't come into it. That's why I'm determined to keep things professional."

"That doesn't sound like much fun." He masks a smile by popping a grape into his mouth.

"Is 'fun' supposed to come into it when you're entrusted with a project that has world-changing potential?" I ask.

"Preferably," Arthur replies, amused. "I am of the personal belief that fun should be had in every serious endeavor. In fact, the more serious a project, the more fun is needed."

I can see he's not joking. I don't know how to respond, so we sit in silence.

"I'm not trying to interfere, or anything," he says finally. "But I would like to tell you something about your new 'colleague.' A few months after his mom died, he joined me and Ambrose as counselors for one of Georgia's ski camps. You should have seen him with that group of kids.

"I don't care how a person acts around their peers or out in public. Get them around a kid who is starved for love, and you will see the 'real' them come out. People either detach and become distant or they open up. And I'm telling you, I've never seen anyone give of himself like Siaka did for those disadvantaged, attention-deprived kids. He was a hero. The real deal.

"So whatever questions you might have…" Arthur looks at me intently, "I can assure you he is worthwhile. The best of people. You can trust him, Louis. Don't let doubt, especially self-doubt, get in the way. If I've learned anything in the last few years, it's been to not let the details get in the way of something profound. Whatever that something may be."

"I don't," I start, but falter. "I'm not sure..."

"Don't respond," he replies. "Just think about it. And now, shouldn't we be getting on with the patient supervision? Because right now, I can feel that cat piss coming back up, and things are about to get ugly."

Chapter Fourteen

The next week races by. Day three after Arthur took the potion, he reported having blurred vision, but admitted it could as easily be attributed to an extra-strenuous workout with Ambrose.

After Arthur's month-long blindness, Bran instated a daily sight test on top of taking pulse, temperature and blood pressure. I recorded this information in the notebook until a few days in, then Liv launched the Beta version of our new communication platform. That meant I could enter the data for Bran and Siaka to check in real time.

I have to hand it to Liv. For a platform created completely from scratch instead of using coding software (thus hack-proof, she claims), it works like a dream.

With much foot-dragging, she labeled the gateway page, "Alliance Network," the official name chosen by Bran and Gaspard. Liv argued it sounded like a Facebook group for World War II buffs and referred to it as "C2C" in her texts and emails.

Siaka finally pried its meaning out of her. "You know B2B communication. Business-to-Business?" she asked. "Well, this is Curers-to-Corpses communication. As in healers and the undead. Close second choice was D2D, Doctors-to-Dead Guys. Get it?"

We got it. And since it was catchier than "Alliance Network," after a few days, C2C stuck.

Since the platform was up, I had no legitimate reason to go to Le Corbeau. I set up an office in a corner of my apartment-sized bedroom and worked by day manually transferring the information from the bardia database to the C2C. At night I would visit my old numa haunts with a few of my kindred, dredging up any useful information I could retrieve from my memories. But most of the time, I was in the library with Gaspard, phoning kindred who hadn't been in touch since the beginning of the Internet, and so had never provided email addresses. To some of these people, a few decades must have been like the blink of an eye.

Meanwhile, Siaka was busy loading the C2C with Flame-finger information. So, a good week goes by with only online communication between us.

Now, every time I think of him, I try to smother my regret with a good dose of reality. We barely spent any time together. Am I so desperate for a boyfriend that I obsess over the first cute I guy meet?

Deep down, I know it's more than that. There's something special about Siaka. If it's due to the close tie between his kind and mine, I have no idea. It's true that most bardia choose a romantic partner from among their own kind—to avoid the situation Arthur and Georgia are in.

But though Siaka bears *the signum bardia* and knows our secrets, and even has supernatural abilities of his own, we aren't the same creature. Like Georgia, he will die one day. I won't—unless I have some very bad luck.

He was friendly toward me, nothing else. What was I thinking to allow myself to crush on him? It was dancing with disaster: idiotic and self-sabotaging.

This is what I tell myself, at least, and it puts me on high alert any time I write him. I read each message carefully before pressing the "send" button, to be sure I don't say anything he can misconstrue. I don't even try to explain my awkwardness again. I simply focus on our project.

And that's my life, besides working out every morning with Ambrose. Sometimes Gaspard joins us. In our three-way spars, I can barely keep up, but I'm getting better every day.

Gaspard has me prioritize Germany and France for the platform, so I begin setting up a secure two-way video link through the C2C. By Friday, it's up and running, and Gaspard calls a house meeting in the basement cinema.

We take our places around a U-shaped table equipped with multiple cameras. Kate and Vincent share one camera, Charlotte and Ambrose share another. Gaspard, Arthur and I each have our own.

As the meeting starts and the mosaic of faces appears on screen one-by-one, the excitement in the room is palpable. Besides bardia from three different locations in Paris and throughout France, we have Charles, Uta, Faust and their clan tuning in from Berlin.

Uta's band of German revenants came to Paris on that fatal day five years ago. It was the afternoon before the Final Battle. The Paris bardia were losing a skirmish against me and my numa clan, when this scary-looking gang of pierced, tatted and fluorescent-haired punks showed up carrying ghetto blasters blaring speed-metal. They turned the tables and won the fight, then hung around La Maison until that night, when they joined Kate and her forces in the Final Battle. So, I had seen enough of them to be prepared for Uta's current look: a swoop of fluorescent green hair and multiple face-piercings.

I've heard of Faust. He accompanied Jules and Ava from New York, where he had been a New York City firefighter who died saving lives on 9/11. The moment Uta laid eyes on him, she decided he was hers. And despite their completely opposite styles (he has that typical "clean-cut bodybuilder" fireman style) they were a match made in...well, La Maison.

But I don't even recognize Charles. The last I saw him he had a lion's mane of black hair with red tips, and now it's a natural-looking golden red and he's sporting a short beard. He still has nose, lip and eyebrow rings, but he's overall less hardcore punk than I remember. He waves to the camera and smiles. "Hi all!"

"Chucky!" Ambrose yells, leaning over to speak directly into the microphone, deafening all of us. "Looking good!"

"You don't have to press your lips to the microphone," Charlotte laughs, clasping his hand on the table. "But I agree, twin—looking good!"

Charles grins. "So do all of you! Hey Louis—welcome!"

"Nice to see you again." I feel suddenly shy. Charles is kind of legendary, both in good and bad ways.

"Shall we commence with the first order of business?" Gaspard skips the niceties and brings the meeting to order.

"It's really the *only* order of business," Kate says. "Our investigation into renewed numa activity in Paris, including our interaction with the Numa Army."

Charles holds up a copy of our photo of the N.A. tattoo. "I did what you asked and had my guys in the ink world spread the word. We got a few responses from tattoo artists claiming they had been asked for a swastika-style tattoo."

"So, this is happening in Germany too?" Kate asks.

Charles shakes his head. "Nope. The artists who got those requests are French. Paris area and to the east, like Reims, Laon…"

"Someone should visit them," Vincent says. "Find the identity of the customers who requested the tattoos."

"Already done!" Charles says. "Henri take the mic."

From another box on the screen, a Paris bardia begins speaking. "Hi Vincent. Kate. Yeah, Charles sent me to question these guys. They were all happy to help. Most of the requests were made by email—people sending the altered swastika image to ask if they could duplicate the tat. Once these artists refused, the issue was dropped. But a few people actually stopped by the tattoo parlors to inquire. Mainly men, but a few women as well. Mostly young. That's the only connection they had—they all looked under thirty.

"One tattoo artist got curious and what the symbol was for. The guy told him it was for an online group. One of these conspiracy theory things. No one's met the leader, who calls himself 'M.' M gives the loyal information and instructs them how to climb the ranks. He says a new order of humans is rising, and that his army will be the first wave."

I glance around the table to gauge the effect of this news. Gaspard looks particularly grim, but the rest seem to be in shock.

Henri continues his story. "This customer confided in the artist that he knew someone who had reached the army's highest level. The guy had done everything M told him to do. And he claimed to have been possessed on several occasions by a higher power that made him stronger and gave him skills he'd never had before. M told him it was in preparation for making him immortal."

There is a moment's silence as everyone digests this information.

Vincent asks, "Where does the tattoo come in?"

"The guy said the tattoo's symbol means that a person has reached Level 5, and that the N.A. stands for 'Numa Army,' which you already discovered."

Gaspard speaks up. "Being possessed by a higher power that grants unprecedented strength and skill…that sounds like possession by a volant revenant."

Kate turns to Vincent. "That's exactly what it felt like when you possessed me so I could kill Lucien. One second, I had no fighting skills. The next you were 'powering' me. Not only showing me what to do but adding your strength to mine so I could wield that heavy sword and throw a knife with enough force to kill him."

"This is starting to make sense," Charlotte says. "Those three bouncers at Judas fought us with numa skills and strength. But when we saw one of them last week, he not only didn't remember fighting me, but didn't remember ever having used a sword. If a numa wanted, it could possess the human in a way he wouldn't remember afterward."

"A numa-organized campaign," Arthur says. "It's genius, really. If they find humans who agree to be possessed by a volant numa spirit, they don't even need to physically enter Paris, where Kate would easily track them by their auras."

"It's like using remote control!" Ambrose agrees. "The numa can make the possessed human do anything they want."

"It has to be small-scale," Vincent muses. "How many numa still exist in our area of France?"

The others look puzzled.

He explains. "A revenant can't be too far away from the human they want to possess. Like maximum a hundred miles. A volant spirit can't just materialize wherever it wants. They have to physically travel to the person. So, these can't be numa spirits from far away flying in to do a job in Paris. Their body has to be located within a hundred miles of Paris. How many can there be, just a few years after we wiped them all out? Not more than a couple dozen at best."

"I agree," Gaspard says. "Depending on who is dormant when, they probably only have a handful of volant spirits they can use at once. Which is enough to carry out a targeted attack, but not to replace all of the numa there used to be in Paris with humans."

"Unless they can actually do what they're saying, and turn these people immortal," Uta jokes. "Because if so, they could build an actual Numa Army like M promises."

"You can't turn a human into a revenant," Charlotte says. "Let's say you manage to manipulate someone into enacting the behavior that leads to a revenant's animation: dying for someone and becoming a bardia. Or dying after betraying someone to their death and becoming a numa. Only a few of these people would have the genetic predisposition, or whatever it is, to become a revenant. Otherwise, you would have a lot of dead humans."

"Unless there was a way to modify a human's genetic makeup to transform them into a latent revenant," Gaspard says. "Which, of course, is ridiculous."

"Oh!" I blurt out, as something dawns on me. A memory is forming from back in my numa days.

"Louis, you're as white as a sheet," Kate says.

"Oh no." I press my fingers hard against my temples. My head swims as a scene from the darkest days of my past returns.

"What is it?" Vincent asks.

"I just remembered something that happened when I was with Violette," I say. "I overheard her talking to Nicolas about working on a way to transform people into revenants."

"What?" Ambrose asks.

"A fairy tale!" Gaspard insists.

"Vi talked about some weird things, but I never heard her talk about that," Arthur says.

"She read about it in an old manuscript," I insist. "Something about a revenant leader in the past who tried to raise an immortal army to fight the Romans. All I can remember is that he had a Flame-finger working on the transformations. Violette wanted to discover that technique and use it to build her numa base."

"Preposterous!" Gaspard exclaims. But there's a look of uncertainty in his eyes, and he starts the nervous fidgeting that has all but disappeared since the first time I met him.

Kate calls for calm. "Okay. This is new knowledge. We need to do more research. Charles, Faust..." Kate lists off several more names. "I want you to find this conspiracy group online and get as much information as you can. Henri, go back to those tattoo artists and see if you can get other leads on people requesting the tattoos. Email addresses, whatever. Gaspard and Louis, I want you to work with Bran and Siaka on tracing this legend about a Flame-finger transforming humans into latent revenants. Sound good?" All nod their assent. "Okay. Thanks everyone. Let's check back in soon."

One by one, the kindred on the screens disappear. Gaspard is already on his phone, and when he hangs up, he turns to me. "Bran will meet us this afternoon in the library." He tucks the phone into his waistcoat and departs, mumbling to himself.

Ambrose pats me on the arm and whispers, "I'm sure we've time for a workout before you start your research."

"I don't know," I reply, not really feeling like it. What I really want is to go straight to my computer and do my own research on this conspiracy group. I'm fascinated and horrified that I might hold the key to this. Maybe something I see will jog my memory.

Ambrose shakes his head and wraps me in his arm-around-the-shoulder death grip. "A workout a day keeps the numa away. Let's go."

Chapter Fifteen

Downstairs in the armory, I duck into a changing room to put on my fighting gear. When I come out, Ambrose is sorting through the weapons racks.

"This one's perfect for your skill level," he says, and hands a sword to someone standing behind him.

He steps aside, and there's Siaka. My heart does a double-flip in my chest, and for a few seconds I forget to breathe.

Siaka looks up and a cautious smile spreads across his face. "Hey, Louis. Thanks for inviting me to work out with you and Ambrose. After a full week of sitting on my butt in front of a computer screen, this is exactly what I needed."

"Um," I say, glancing at Ambrose. His mischievous smile and raised eyebrow tell me everything I need to know. Because I sure didn't invite Siaka. After our last prickly encounter, I wouldn't have dared. "No problem. It's good to see you again."

"Choose your weapon. Siaka's on sword, I'm on battle-axe, obviously," Ambrose says.

"Sword's good for me," I reply, as if it doesn't make a difference. But I choose the sword I know I'll handle best while Ambrose puts some battle-worthy music on the sound system.

The three-way skirmishes I've had with Gaspard and Ambrose were physically difficult. Both are masters of the art and clearly held back in speed and force to allow me to keep up. Even then, they pushed me to my limit.

This is different. Ambrose and Gaspard are kindred—Ambrose like an older brother, and Gaspard an eccentric uncle. But Siaka… He's *way* outside my comfort zone. I'm super self-conscious that I'm doing badly—very badly. My reactions are slow and I'm hesitant to hit him hard. "This isn't working," I say after a few minutes.

"It's probably me," Siaka says. "It's been a month since I worked out with a weapon."

"No," I say, "You're really good. I didn't know you trained."

His face lights up. "Yeah, Gaspard's been training me for two years now. I don't know about *good*, but I'm better."

"No, seriously. Respect," I say. "The problem is totally me. My rhythm's off." *And with good reason*, I think as I try not to stare at the defined muscles under Siaka's close-fitting T-shirt.

In a swift set of movements, Ambrose tosses his axe onto its pegs, takes the swords from us, and replaces them with long wooden sticks.

"We're switching to quarterstaffs," he says. "You guys aren't used to fighting each other. You're holding back. These'll do the trick. Hit each other as hard as you want, and all you'll get is a bruise. Or, maybe a broken arm," he says, pausing to consider the potential extent of quarterstaff damage. "Let's focus on hitting and blocking, but not smashing."

We start again.

This time I get into the rhythm—hitting, blocking, sweeping low to trip my opponent, jumping when Ambrose or Siaka does the same. We start slow, then accelerate. Swinging, swooping, blocking…our staffs form arcs and lines until I can almost see an intricate net of invisible forms carved out of the armory air.

I discover that when I concentrate on completing the shapes we draw instead of finding the right move, I'm free to go all-out. I feel stronger and more agile. Our moves match the music's beat, and I get flashes of my opponents' expressions between strikes. Ambrose's intense concentration broken by flashes of exuberance when he executes the perfect sequence. Siaka's single-minded focus, punctuated with exuberant yells. A few times, between strikes, our eyes meet. He's radiating pure enjoyment. Anything I said or did to hurt his feelings is forgotten.

After a half hour of intense combat, Siaka lowers his quarterstaff and puts a hand up. "Break! I call break!" he pants.

"I hoped you'd say that," I utter, gasping for breath. Setting down my weapon, I lean over, propping myself up, giving my racing heart a chance to return to normal rhythm.

"I'm dripping with sweat." Siaka rips off his T-shirt, leaving only a pair of white canvas judo pants, bare feet, and a perfectly chiseled chest. His skin glows under the overhead lights. My adrenaline-fueled high evaporates and I feel suddenly weak.

Ambrose stands there in tank top and shorts, grinning and twirling the heavy quarterstaff like it's a toy baton. His weightlifting champion body, muscles bulging, couldn't be more of a contrast to Siaka's toned, balanced physique.

"The newbies need a break," Ambrose teases, strutting back and forth with the quarterstaff. "That's okay, man. But in a few years, none of this break stuff. Nope. In a few years, I will have no more mercy on your fragile chicken butts. Ambrose, the master of the workout, the unstoppable…"

His pump-up speech is interrupted by a voice from the top of the stairs.

"Ambrose! Cupcake! I have that thing I need you to help me with," Charlotte calls.

This knocks Ambrose out of his zone. "Can it wait?"

"No," she says. "It's that *thing*. Remember?"

He remembers. Dropping the testosterone-fueled diatribe, he channels a twelve-year-old who's in on a joke. "Oh, right!" he responds. "The *thing*! Be right there."

"Sorry, guys," he says, fitting his quarterstaff onto its wall hooks. "Promised to help the wifie with a *thing*. But feel free to stay down here and keep sparring. If you want. Or you could maybe *talk*. You know, whatever."

He's up the stairs and the door slams. Now, it's just the two of us.

"Um, that was…" I begin.

"So obvious," Siaka says, laughing.

"Obviously a plot to get the two of us together. Word must have spread that things aren't exactly working between the two of us."

Siaka shakes his head, but is still smiling, "These guys are always way up in each other's business. No privacy at all. Water?"

We hang our quarterstaffs on the wall rack and head toward the watercooler. Filling two sports bottles with ice-cold water, we slump down across from each other on overstuffed white couches in a corner of the room.

Siaka blots his face with a towel and hangs it around his neck. "So," he begins.

"So," I reply, tipping water onto my towel and dabbing my face with it. I lean back and sprawl in a position that I hope looks casual, never taking my eyes off him. "I think I should start."

"Be my guest."

"You totally misunderstood when I..." He tenses up in defensiveness, and I change my tactic. "Living in semi-isolation for the last five years has made me the suckiest person imaginable for communicating. Like, I put my foot in my mouth every time I open it."

He nods. "Carry on."

"So, if it sounded like I was inferring in any way that I think bardia are superior to Flame-fingers, or that you are here to serve us, or whatever shit actually came out of my mouth, I want you to know...I didn't mean it."

He starts to say something, but I hold my hand up. "Because—and I'm saying this with one hundred percent sincerity—I am in total awe of you and Bran and what you're doing. And what you're *capable* of doing. I'm not even a full-fledged bardia yet, but when I am, that won't change my view of you and your kind. From what Gaspard says, Flame-fingers and revenants have been living symbiotically since the dawn of time. We need you and you need us. I'm not really clear on *how* you need us, but..."

"Because the purpose of *guérriseurs* in general is to save humanity from illness, pain, whatever," he explains. "Your purpose as bardia is to save humanity from death. You advance our cause with your own mission, by doing something we're unable to do. And the Flame-fingers, we *guérriseurs* who heal bardia, facilitate your mission by keeping your kind running as smoothly as possible. You don't help us personally, unless you happen to save one of us in the course of your work. But you help us professionally, to achieve our goal of healing humanity."

Siaka says all of this as if it were common sense. I imagine his mother teaching him, using the same exact words. Like her mother taught her. And so on. The idea is so ingrained in him that it seems like basic logic.

"So, we can agree that our people are equals," I say. "But I wouldn't even dare to say that about you and me."

He looks at me quizzically.

"You are so much more advanced than I am," I clarify. "You've been studying this stuff since you were a kid. You've had the best teachers possible, being mentored by your mom and then Bran. You're smart, you've got your shit together, and you're…" My eyes stray from his face to his chest, and I totally lose the thread of what I'm trying to say. I squeeze my eyes shut. "You're totally distracting. Could you…put a shirt on?"

Oh no, I think. *I just ruined everything.* My blood temperature dives to subzero, freezing in my veins. I feel like crying. Or hiding. But when I open an eye to measure the extent of damage I've done, Siaka is staring at me with an expression of astonishment, which is quickly replaced by a look of proud amusement. "Distracting? Really?" He glances down at his naked, perfect torso.

I shield my eyes with a hand, masking my embarrassment. "Really."

"So, when you were acting all stand-offish and cold, that wasn't because you didn't like working with me?"

I look him in the eyes. "No. I love working with you. I love being around you. Hanging out with you is the most fun I've had in years. But I can't help liking you as more than a colleague."

Now he's grinning. "Oh yeah?"

There's something about him that makes my words keep flowing. Instead of sticking to the necessary, everything's pouring out. "When you electrify me with your touch, I know it's the Flame-finger–bardia connection. But it's not uncomfortable, like you said it was for the others. It's like…"

Like what? I think. *Are you going to say this?* Well, yes, my mouth keeps moving, so obviously I am. "It's like I don't want you to stop."

"You mean, like this?" Reaching out, Siaka touches my arm with his fingertips. A current of excitement, and desire, and something deeper courses through me. I'm looking straight into his eyes as his fingers press my skin, and all I want to do is lean forward and kiss him. My eyes skim down to his lips, and it takes all my strength to pull my arm away and say, "Stop."

The electrified pressure of his fingers disappears, and along with it the overwhelming emotions. I take a deep breath and say, "Now please, for the love of god, put a shirt on."

He laughs, walks away, and comes back wearing a hoodie.

"Thank you."

"No problem," he chuckles. "So, my touch is too intense for you?"

"Um, yeah. You can't imagine…"

"Actually, I can," he says. His lips curl up in a mischievous smile. "Let's just say, I'm equally affected. Not by the touch, but by you."

My mind hits this speedbump and sends me flying. It's a good ten seconds before I can speak as I process this information. "Wait…you are?"

"Why do you think I offered to pick you up on the scooter those times? It would have been easier for you to take the Métro."

"You feel…?" I'm unsure how to finish.

"Yep," he says. "That's why it hurt extra-bad when I thought you didn't want to work with me. Or worse, didn't respect me." He looks thoughtful. "Seems like we're in a predicament."

I nod. "We can't do this. We can't like each other. We have to work together. Everyone's counting on us. What if something actually happened and it became more than just *like*?"

"It would be awesome," he says, completing my thought, "until there was a problem."

"Exactly! That's exactly what I'm thinking. We're in this thing together. We're representing our people. If we let personal stuff come between us—if we broke up, or did something that hurt the other, and then had to keep showing up to work? It could be…" I was going to say "heartbreaking" but then I remembered my sister calling me a drama queen and swap the word for "painful."

He reaches forward and takes my hand in his. The current is still there, but now that we've identified it, it's more bearable. "So, it looks like we're going to have to agree not let it go beyond the 'like' stage."

"Looks like it," I agree, and catching his eyes, see something that reminds me of Arthur's story. I see Siaka's goodness. And it makes me happy that I was chosen to work with him. That I have all this time in the future to spend in his presence. That, in itself, feels like a gift. I shouldn't need more.

"So, we can hang out outside of work," I begin.

"We *should*," he says. "We need to know each other better to avoid more of these misunderstandings."

"Definitely," I agree. "What do you like to do?"

He's silent for a moment, thinking, then his eyes light up. "Hey, I know! We're both from Paris, but you haven't been here for five years. Let's take turns choosing a place we don't think the other person's been to. Something secret or out of the way."

"Or maybe so obvious that we haven't ever bothered to go?" I add.

We smile at each other and both say, "The Eiffel Tower."

"Okay, I'm going to add to that 'doing something we've never done,'" I say, the spark of an idea forming in my mind. "So it doesn't have to be location-specific. But since it was your idea, you have to start first. I'll need more time to come up with a plan."

"I've got the perfect place in mind," he says, grinning. "Are you free tomorrow night?"

"They don't really need me any more on patrol," I say. "Charlotte thinks we've exhausted leads from my numa hangouts, and Kate says my time is better spent on research."

"I'll help with the research," he says, "if it could earn us some hang time."

Seeing his smile, I make a resolution. If it takes forcing a platonic friendship to keep this person in my life every day, then so be it.

I go to the place in my mind where, despite myself, a little seed of hope has been growing, pushing its way toward warm sunlight. I pluck it by its roots and crush it between my fingers. There is pain, but not as much as if I had let it bloom.

I squeeze Siaka's hand in mine, and then let it go. "It's a deal."

Chapter Sixteen

Siaka and I knuckle down and make huge advances on the database. However, with our attempts to dig up online information about the Numa Army, their tattoos, or conspiracy groups that resemble M's, we discover nothing new. Three days of non-stop work later, Bran and Gaspard urge us to take some time off. We jump at the offer.

We're standing outside of a row of identical one-story buildings with pointed roofs. They look like Monopoly houses, but instead of green plastic they're made of brown stone. Just above doorway-height, arched niches run the length of the buildings. In each one is a creepy white plaster head. I recognize Jacques Chirac, Frankenstein and Batman.

"Um," is the only comment I can formulate.

Siaka laughs. "Those were plaster casts used to make party masks. When the mask factory closed, this guy Favand bought them and put them here so they wouldn't be destroyed. The Museum of Fairground Arts contains his collection of antiques from old amusement parks."

"What, like merry-go-rounds?" I cast around in my mind for what someone could collect from old amusement parks and come up with antique clown statues, derelict haunted house rides, and leering carnival barkers. None of which are reassuring.

"Oh, so much more," Siaka responds. "But no spoilers. You've got to see it yourself." He locks our helmets beneath the scooter's seat and pockets the keys. How can he make such an ordinary gesture look completely hot? I squeeze my eyes shut to erase the image of Sexy Siaka and hope when I open them it'll be Colleague Siaka standing there, just another teenage guy, totally unhot. I open my eyes. It didn't work. He's smiling at me, totally adorable, and touches me on the arm—which sends all my crush-resisting resolve straight to hell.

I try to focus on his words as we approach the entrance.

"There's a guided tour, but I've been so many times, I've got it down by heart."

"Awesome!" I deadpan. "My own personal guide on the creepiest tour ever."

He laughs. "Let's go."

He presents his phone to the woman taking tickets, then leads me under an arched doorway overgrown with ivy. We find ourselves in a courtyard enclosed by a second row of Monopoly houses built behind the ones facing the street.

"These used to be old wine storage warehouses," Siaka says, starting the tour, "when Bercy was still considered its own village outside of Paris. That's what the train tracks are for," he says, pointing to old rails embedded in the cobblestone. "Train cars transported the wine into Paris, where it was taxed. So, everyone came out to here to party on cheap, untaxed wine outside the city limits.

"But when Bercy was swallowed up by the city, these buildings were abandoned, and Jean Paul Favand bought them to house his collection of performing and fairground arts."

"Wow, you really know your stuff," I say.

"Just wait. You'll see why I love it so much," Siaka promises.

We head through a door at one end of the interconnected warehouses and begin walking through rooms packed with the most astounding, beautiful and downright weird objects that could possibly be assembled under one roof. We pass a couple of tour groups led by official guides, but head off to be on our own.

We walk up to a mannequin composed of a woman's body with a unicorn head. It wears an old-fashioned nightgown and stands next to a grand piano like it's about to belt out a solo. "This is like being in a nightmare," I say, genuinely freaked out.

"Funny you say that," Siaka laughs. "It was honest-to-god used in a horror novel about nightmares. Authors treat this place like an inspiration playground." He takes my hand and pulls me past the creeptastic unicorn.

"This is only the beginning," I hear him say, but I lose all focus because he takes my hand in his. All I can think about are his short-cropped curls and how I want to run my fingers through them.

We arrive at a vintage fairground game: a ten-foot-tall backdrop painted as though it's the inside of an old café. A troupe of metal waiters holding trays aloft are grouped at one end, and the goal is to race them horizontally across the tableau to a finish line at the far end of the café. In front of the set-up are twelve mini-bowling alleys with a pyramid of holes instead of bowling pins, and in front of the bowling alleys are twelve stools.

"It's like Skee-ball," Siaka says, dropping my hand and settling onto the furthest stool. I take the one next to him, and six other visitors eagerly plant themselves on the others. "You take the wooden balls and roll them up into the holes. Each hole counts a different number of points and moves your waiter forward."

An attendant starts the game. With the rolling of the wooden balls and the excited cries of the participants, the noise is deafening. I grab each ball as it rolls toward me and spin it up the alley toward the elusive top hole, worth fifty points. I haven't done anything like this since I was a kid, and in seconds revert to eight-year-old me, yelling and jumping with the rest of the players. In the end, Siaka's tray-carrying, white-aproned waiter crosses the finish line first.

"Yes!" he yells, leaping up and pumping his fist.

"Wait a minute. How many times have you played this?"

"Doesn't matter," he says. "That there was pure skill."

"Why do I get the feeling you come here on your free time just to practice?"

He holds up his hands and wiggles his fingers. "Maybe it's a Flame-finger superpower."

We move on to a velocipede carousel where, instead of horses, bikes are positioned around the edge of a merry-go-round. "In the late nineteenth century, these carousels were the only way many people could afford to try a bicycle," Siaka explains. "As a publicity stunt, the fairground manager had a team of firemen test how fast it would go. They got up to thirty-seven miles per hour—faster than most people had ever gone other than on horseback."

After climbing aboard my own bike and beginning to pedal, I discover just how fast it goes. At one point, I lift my feet. The pedals are moving so fast I can't put them back down.

After the bike carousel, we pass displays of mechanical player pianos, costumes from the Moulin Rouge, and a whole battalion of terrifying mechanized mannequins and figurines. It sounds like a dozen possessed music boxes are playing carnival tunes.

The last attraction is a "gondola" merry-go-round, a circular platform set with a couple dozen colorful wooden swans, ducks and two-seated booths. Siaka and I wedge ourselves side-by-side into a booth so small that we're practically crushed together, which I don't mind one bit.

Siaka turns to me. "This ride seems more your speed. You're looking less green."

I elbow him playfully, instigating a shoving battle, ending only when I grab his hands to stop him from pushing me out of the booth. Which results in us sitting there, my hands on his and our faces an inch apart.

For one charged moment, I seriously consider kissing him. His lips are right there. His eyes tease me. It takes all of my will-power to disengage. I let go of his hands and lean back.

"So…" he says, pursing his lips. "How about that C2C database?"

We both burst into laughter, and when the gondola ride comes to a stop we climb out and leave the museum with smiles that won't go away.

Chapter Seventeen

It's my turn to choose an activity for the next week, but a few hours after dropping me off from the Museum of Fairground Arts, Siaka calls. He explains that Liv needs to take the database offline to fix some bugs.

"She says sooner rather than later. If we tell her to do it tomorrow, that gives us the day off, but it means two dates in a row."

"*Dates?*" I ask pointedly.

"Platonic get-togethers," he corrects.

"Well, I've already decided what to do for my…platonic get-together," I say. "I'll see if I can make it happen tomorrow."

After checking in with Ambrose, I call Siaka back.

"Okay, but it has to be before sunrise," I say. "Which doesn't bother me since I don't sleep. Think you can make it?"

"That sounds like an immortal-to-mortal challenge," Siaka says. "How can I say no?"

The next morning at five a.m., he meets me on the quai next to Pont Royal bridge. Ambrose is there, having helped me drag a pile of equipment down the stone stairway from his jeep. "Better suit up," he tells Siaka. "The Seine's a bit chilly this early in the day."

"Wait what?" Siaka looks alarmed. Then he notices the full wetsuit I'm wearing, and the material spread out on the quai, and his expression is split between astonishment and skepticism. "Stand-up paddling on the Seine? Is this even legal?"

"Ambrose called his police contacts, and they gave us special permission as long as we finish before the riverboats start up at sunrise. That gives us two hours."

Siaka studies the equipment as though it might bite him. "I'm not sure…"

"Come on!" I plead. "There's your wetsuit. If you're not too shy, just strip down to your underwear and put it on. I swear I won't look."

From his change in expression, I see that challenging Siaka is the best way to motivate him. Turning my back and giving him privacy to get dressed, I sit down on the edge of the quai and pull wetsuit boots over my bare feet.

"I can't believe I'm doing this," he mumbles, as I hear him unzip his jeans and shuffle into the neoprene suit.

"Have you ever stand-up paddled?" I call over my shoulder.

"Nope." There's a trace of anxiety in his voice.

"You just have to keep your balance," I reassure him. "Since the paddle boards are big and heavy, they're hard to flip. It's easier than it looks."

"Says the guy who spent the last five years surfing off Brittany's coast."

I hear him zip the front of his suit and turn around. "As I remember, you're the one who set the not-a-date dating rules. It has to be a place you've never been to or a thing you've never done. This qualifies, no?"

He presses his fingers to his temples. "You've got me there. Okay. Let's do this thing!"

After ten minutes, and some minimal instruction, we are upright on our boards, paddles in hand, rowing our way toward the Eiffel Tower. The sun hasn't risen, so the tower lights are still on. And as cheesy-touristy as the Eiffel Tower usually feels, seeing it lit up like a steampunk Christmas tree, lights reflecting off the water's surface, waves rippling all around us…well, it's downright magical.

Siaka takes no time to get his balance. Within minutes, he is navigating steadily enough to pull up from behind and paddle next to me. "I'm going to focus on the water's reflection," he says, "because if I look up, I'll fall in."

"Then sit down on the board," I suggest. "That's what you do when you want to rest."

Grasping the edges of the boards for balance, we lower ourselves into seated positions. I have him extend one end of his paddle to me, then give him the end of mine, so our boards are connected. We float side-by-side, bobbing on the waves while looking up at "La Dame de Fer," as the Parisians call *La Tour Eiffel*.

"This is bad. This is really, really bad," Siaka says in a low voice.

"Why?" I search his face for what could possibly be wrong.

"I'll have to up my game if I'm going to beat floating on the Seine at daybreak."

I grin. "Just keeping you on your toes."

He reaches out, across the water, for my hand. We lock gazes, and I am struck by the desire once again, this time searingly strong, to get as close to him as possible.

"Holding hands is alright between us. Right?" His eyes flash with amusement.

"Totally," I reply, with all the false confidence I can muster. "Hand-holding's nothing like kissing. Still extremely platonic."

"Extremely?"

"Slightly platonic," I correct.

"It's a good thing we've got a few inches of polluted river water between us."

"Yeah, wouldn't want to risk falling in." I give in and let myself stare at his lips. They are full and soft, and I want to press them with my own.

He gives me a knowing grin. "Nope. Not taking any risks."

We fall silent and hold hands, gazing up at the tower.

This is as close to perfect as I think I'll ever find. Me, Siaka and the quiet lapping of the water against our boards. Just…perfect.

Chapter Eighteen

We could sit in silence for another hour before heading back, but there's so much I want to know about him. Still, bobbing on boards in the middle of Seine, nothing seems serious, and I feel the courage to ask him the questions I've been pondering.

"Were you born here or in Mali?" I begin.

"Here." He shifts his gaze from the tower to my eyes, and letting go of my hand, leans back on his elbows. I keep a grip on the paddle so we won't drift apart. "My mom and her sister came from Mali when they were in their twenties."

I settle back to listen. Finally, I'm getting his story.

He looks back toward the twinkling tower. "My mom's family lived on the Niger River in a village known for its pottery. Her people had been *guérisseurs* in that area for generations. Several of my ancestors were called upon to heal important people—kings even—and had been offered palaces to stay in. But after healing each patient, they always came back home, no matter what riches they were offered.

"Mom said our village was built upon a place of strength. Bran once talked to me about energy centers. His house is built on one, near ancient dolmens. The village was a place like that. Mom said that it was the source of their healing powers."

I nudge his foot with mine, and he reaches over to touch my hand. I ignore the fireworks and wait for him to continue.

"My mother's father, a fisherman, died in a river accident just after she was born, so my *guérriseur* grandmother raised the two girls by herself. She was well-respected in the region, and the village chief let her do things her own way. But she got sick and before she died, she passed the gift on to my mother, who was twenty-three. At that point, the chief decided he wanted to control my mom's power. He thought he could marry her and charge people for her services. Can you imagine?"

I can't.

"The sisters fled in the night. In Bamako, they looked up a contact their mother had given them in case if they were ever in trouble. It was a wealthy businessman she had brought back from the brink of death. The man was so grateful that he arranged for my mom and her sister to travel to Paris. He found them lodging and jobs."

Siaka stops, lost in thought.

"How did she meet your dad?" I prompt. "If he's Bran's cousin, that means he's from a *guérriseur* family too."

"They met through Le Corbeau," he replies. "Mom said she was called to it. She was passing by, and something drew her inside. Gwenaëlle, Bran's mother, was in the shop that day. She saw the tattoo that my grandmother had inked on my mother's hand and recognized her as a fellow Flame-finger. She took the sisters in like they were family. It was just a matter of time before my mom met my dad at a family gathering in Brittany."

"Good story," I say.

He smiles sadly and nods.

"Do you have the same tattoo as your mother?"

"Didn't you notice the other day in the armory?" he replies with a cheeky grin. Sitting up, he unzips his wetsuit. "I asked Mom to put it near my heart."

There, perfectly centered over his sternum, is a hand, palm-forward with a flame topping each finger. It's inked in a series of small dots, as if done by individual needle-pricks.

"Do you have any tattoos?" he asks.

My heart drops. "Nothing worth seeing."

"Wait…what?" He shifts to turn toward me. "You have a secret tattoo and it's not worth seeing? Come on. Now you have to show me."

"Seriously, Siaka. It's no big deal." My face is burning.

"What? You got something stupid that you regret? I know this guy who got a toilet tattooed on his arm on a dare during a drinking game. It can't be worse than that, can it?"

"Actually, it can," I say.

"Worse than a toilet?"

He's not going to give up. So I unzip the top of my wetsuit and pull it down to expose my shoulder.

He looks confused, trying to work out why I have a tattoo of a small purple flower encased in a letter V. His face transforms as he gets it. "Oh my god, did she force you to get that?"

My mouth is too dry to speak.

"You were thirteen years old, and Violette forced you to get a tattoo with her emblem?"

There is so much pity in his voice that I can't look him in the eye. I pull the suit back up and zip it.

"You can have it removed," he says.

"I've tried. Three times. It comes back each time I go dormant. You know, when our bodies are supposed to be healing themselves. Bran says that because it was done after my human self died, it's here to stay."

Now I'm the one staring at the tower. I don't want to see Siaka's expression. He knows my shameful secret. The secret that stayed with me long after my acts were forgiven and my numa aura disappeared. The one I will carry through all my afterlifes.

A minute passes. Or maybe fifteen. I don't feel time. All I can feel is pain.

Siaka shifts his board over, and his hand closes over mine. The electricity in his touch goes straight to my heart and reaches that gaping wound. And for some reason—whether Flame-finger magic or just plain human compassion—the pain fades a little. I close my eyes, and we sit holding hands until the sun rises.

Chapter Nineteen

After our two non-dates, I can't justify more time off. We leave the timing for our next meeting open and dive back into our work. Liv has finished her database updates, and we spend the next day playing catch-up with the entries. It seems we're done with angst, and our communication stays lighthearted, aided by a running conversation on C2C's instant messenger that has nothing to do with bardia or Flame-fingers.

Siaka: Butt still frozen from sitting in ice-cold Seine this morning.

Me: There was 5mm of neoprene between said butt and river. That's almost the thickest wetsuit possible!

Him: I've got a Malian butt. It's used to warm weather.

Me: I promise to take your butt's ideal temperature into consideration for my next date plan.

Him: Date?

Me: Friendly excursion.

Him: Will platonic hand-holding be involved in said excursion?

Me: I sure as hell hope so.

Him: *Halo smiley face.*

That afternoon I take a break and head down to the kitchen. There's a French tradition called *le goûter* where all French kids have their afternoon snack, necessary since dinner isn't usually served until seven-thirty at the earliest.

As I enter the kitchen, my senses are flooded by the warmth of the oven and the buttery smell of freshly-baked pastries. Jeanne is loading up a cooling rack with *chouquettes*, which are hollow golf-ball-sized pastries coated with sugar crystals. When you buy them at the *patisserie*, they're good. But when you eat them still warm, just out of the oven, they are melt-in-your-mouth delicious. I take a bite of one of Jeanne's and practically swoon.

"I see you approve," she says, smiling. "You better get yourself a plateful before Ambrose finds out they're ready!"

I load up a plate with pastries, grab a banana off the fruit bowl, make myself a coffee, and sit down at the table to dig in.

Georgia and Arthur make their way into the kitchen, proving that, even though *goûter* is for kids, it is an unspoken tradition for adults as well. They take four or five *chouquettes* each and join me at the table.

"I need to do today's check-up," I remind Arthur. "I can come down later."

"No need," Arthur says. "You can just write down in your book that since yesterday, I can't taste anything,"

I look at his full plate of *chouquettes*.

"Doesn't mean I'm not hungry," he says, and pops one in his mouth.

"So, you'll be coming along tonight, of course," Georgia tells, not asks.

"Um, sure?" I venture. I have no idea what she's talking about.

"Great!" She smiles beatifically at Jeanne, who sets a sugar bowl and pitcher of milk next to her coffee. "Jeanne, if you could possibly take care of Odette tonight, Vincent can join us."

"Vincent already asked me," Jeanne responds. "He and Kate will be joining you—Kate only in spirit, of course, since she's volant today—and I will be babysitting Odette."

"Awesome. Thank you so much!" Georgia says. Crunching through a crispy pastry shell, she rolls her eyes in pleasure. "Oh my god, best *chouquettes* in Paris," she moans.

Jeanne gives a satisfied smile and turns back to the oven.

"So, where exactly are we going tonight?" I ask.

Georgia's mouth full, she tries sign language, but Arthur answers. "Georgia's ex-boyfriend Sebastien and his group have a concert tonight."

"So we're all taking a break from Numa Army surveillance?" I ask.

Arthur shakes his head. "Not all. Charlotte and Ambrose will be visiting an eastern suburb with our Mouzaïa house. Georgia and I are meeting them after the concert. Vincent's on Dad duty. And Gaspard wants you on the database tonight but said you might enjoy coming with us to the concert first."

Gaspard is right. The last few days of having some down time has done wonders for my mental health. "Can I bring a friend?"

Instead of answering, Georgia picks up her phone. Scrolling through her contacts, she dials. "Hey Siaka?" she says, winking at me. "Wanna come to a concert tonight? Nine p.m. at New Morning." She pauses. "By the way, Louis's coming. Great! See you there."

She hangs up, gives a Cheshire Cat grin and bites into a *chouquette.*

"I guess that answers your question," Arthur says, looking thoroughly amused.

Feeling my cheeks redden, I rise to take my dishes to the sink. The kitchen doors fly open and Ambrose barges in, looking like he heard it was the Apocalypse. "Kate told me I better hurry or there wouldn't be any *chouquettes* left."

"Don't worry, *ma puce*," Jeanne says, patting him on the arm. "I have a whole tray reserved just for you, coming out of the oven in a couple of minutes."

Ambrose breathes a sigh of relief and sits down at the head of the table. Jeanne places a tumbler of milk in front of him, and he drains it in one go.

"See you tonight," I say to Georgia.

"Dress nice," she replies. "And by nice, I mean hot."

I shake my head and leave the kitchen.

***

It's roasting hot in the concert hall. My mouth is parched and sweat beads on my forehead as the warm-up group finishes its act. Georgia steers us to the bar just before the last song ends. Arthur, Vincent and I are standing at the front of the drink line, when I feel Kate speaking into my mind.

Guess who's about to arrive?

Even though she's volant, I can tell she's teasing me.

"How is it that *everyone* at La Maison is aware of my *completely innocent* crush?" I murmur, knowing she can hear me despite the cacophony of voices and music.

How could anyone not *know?* Her words come straight into my brain.

"You know I'm a blusher," I say, "so that's just mean. I thought you were on my side."

I've been Team Louis the whole way, she says. It's just that shipping Team Louaka is so much more entertaining.

"LOUAKA?" I say out loud. "Oh my god. Are you kidding?"

Then I shut up because here he comes, making his way through the crowd, hotness incarnate. Liv follows, her hair braided in cornrows that end halfway down her back. She texts as she walks, not bothering to look up and check out the space.

Siaka smiles as he spots me. My heart performs a crazy jackknife in my chest. I call over the crowd, "What do you want to drink?"

He shakes his head and points to his ear—*Can't hear!*—so I mime drinking out of a soda can. "Perrier!" he yells back, pointing between him and Liv.

Having finally reached the bartender, I order for us while Arthur gets beer for him and Vincent, and Diet Coke for Georgia.

Siaka reaches us and there are *bises* all around, even from Liv who deigns to look up from her phone to give a bored kiss to each cheek presented to her.

"Her boyfriend's supposed to be meeting us," Siaka explains, looking apologetic. He takes a sip of Perrier. "Nice T-shirt," he says, wedging himself in next to me as we shove our way toward the stage.

I glance down at the vintage Nirvana T-shirt that, I have to say, fits me perfectly.

"Georgia insisted on dressing me," I admit. "Between her, Charlotte and Jeanne all plotting to take over my wardrobe and social life, I feel like I'm living in a house full of moms."

"Lucky," Siaka says, and there's a hint of wistfulness beneath the jokiness that makes me realize I'm fortunate to have so many people who care about me on a daily basis. He only has his dad—when he's around—and Bran, who, though he has his good qualities, isn't exactly gushing with warmth and affection.

It dawns on me that I'm finally beginning to get what I so desperately longed for.

Acceptance.

Belonging.

My smile widens to match Siaka's. He motions to his shirt. "I don't go to many concerts. So, I thought that a plain old T-shirt would be the safest."

Nothing he wears could be plain or old, I think. The shirt's the same shade of green as his eyes. It's in a cotton that looks so soft, I want to run my hands all over it. I sip my Perrier to distract myself.

"So, is he coming?" Siaka yells, turning to Liv.

"Working late." She frowns at her screen. "He might try to catch the end of the concert." She looks like she regrets having tagged along.

"You into music?" I ask her, trying to make conversation.

For a second, she looks like she's going to say something sarcastic, then she tips her head to the side and nods.

"I guess Sebastien's band is supposed to be 'New Grunge,'" I say, using finger quotes.

"Thus, the classic grunge shout-out." She eyes my T-shirt.

"It's actually Georgia's," I say.

"That makes sense." She glances at Arthur, who's standing right beside me talking to Vincent. "Her boyfriend looks like a non-druggy version of Kurt Cobain."

I turn to stare at Arthur. "Wow, you're right!"

Liv lifts her eyebrows and shrugs, as if, *Of course I'm right. When have I ever not been?*

The next band starts pulling out their equipment, and Georgia jumps up on stage with them. She whispers something into a tall, slim guy's ear then gives him an excited hug.

Arthur turns to me. "Remember what we talked about the other day?"

"Georgia's not wanting to be *anyone's anything*?" I reply.

He grins and tips his head toward the stage. "*That* is her showing me she's a free agent."

"You don't seem to mind." I'm impressed by his coolness.

"That punk's only been around twenty-five years. I have centuries of experience on him. I know how to show Georgia what she's worth. Which makes me confident. And confidence is always sexy." As if hearing his words, Georgia gives us a wave, keeping one arm around Sebastian.

Arthur blows her a lazy kiss, then turns back to me, completely unbothered by her flirting. "One. Two. Three," he counts slowly. By the count of four, Georgia has hopped off the stage and is on her toes, planting a kiss on Arthur's cheek.

"Seb's so glad you came," she says to him, and then looks around at us to extend the compliment to the group.

"I'm sure those were his very words," Arthur says, as Sebastian stares out at us, annoyed.

"Well, his group must be good. This place is packed," Siaka tells Georgia.

He's right. It's standing room only and people are jammed in. The place is thick with the smell of beer and body odor.

As if reading my mind, one of the bouncers opens a side-door to let some air in. I see a couple of guys walk up to ask him something. He nods, and they step outside to light cigarettes.

There's something familiar about them, but I can't quite place where I've seen them. I'm distracted by Vincent, who's saying that the last time they came to one of Sebastien's concerts they were attacked by numa afterward. When I look back at the guys, they're staring directly at Liv, and it clicks.

I lean towards Siaka and motion toward the exit door. "Aren't those the burnouts who were smoking behind Liv's squat?"

"God damn it," Liv mutters, reading a text. "Reese isn't coming." She sees us staring at the door and cranes her head to see what we're looking at. The burnout guys duck out of sight.

"Liv, did you invite some guys from your squat?" Siaka asks.

"I didn't invite anyone but Reese," she replies. "What are you guys staring at?"

"Those two jerk-face stoners who were in the courtyard behind your building the other day. They're here, at the concert. When you looked up, they hid." Siaka's says.

"What do they look like?" Liv asks, with a glimmer of interest.

"Redhead-beard guy and dark-haired beard guy," I say. "Skinny. In their twenties."

"Oh, them." She rolls her eyes. "They're probably just catching the concert like us. But they're hiding because I called them out for being wank-face misogynistic dicks in front of the whole building."

Siaka and I share a worried glance. We're interrupted by Sebastien, who starts talking from the stage, his lips smashed against the microphone. "Hey Paris. We're the Bleeding Heart-Fingers." His band launches into a crashing wall of noise making further discussion impossible.

I glance at the emergency exit and see that the bouncer ushered the smokers back in and closed the door behind them.

The redhead raises his arm to point at the band and yells something stupid like, "Rock and roll!" And that's when I see the tattoo on the back of his bicep. It's a three-armed swastika with the letters "N.A." underneath.

"Kate!" I say, but I don't sense her nearby. I grab Vincent's arm. "Where's Kate?" I yell right next to his head.

He flinches and rubs his ear. "There's some major police activity down the street. She's checking it out."

"A guy over there has a Numa Army tattoo," I yell, and suddenly I have his total attention.

"Where?" he asks.

Arthur, sensing our alarm, turns to include himself in the conversation.

"Next to the emergency exit," I motion. "Guy with the red manbun and beard."

"Stay here with Georgia," Arthur orders, his laid-back coolness evaporating in a split second. He and Vincent surge through the crowd. They haven't gotten more than a few feet when the two guys notice they've been spotted.

Turning, Dark Beard rears back and punches the bouncer in the face. While the guy is reeling, they shove past him and out the emergency exit. The bouncer lunges after them, yelling. Arthur and Vincent follow, and the door slams behind them. It happens so quickly that only the people immediately around the door notice.

"Hey, where'd Arthur go?" Georgia yells, having stopped dancing long enough to notice he's gone.

"He and Vincent went to check something outside. They'll be right back," I say. She looks unhappy but turns and waves her arms to the beat. I look at Siaka like, *What now?* He shrugs, and we try to get back into the music. The second song ends, and Sebastien drones on about his inspiration for the next song.

Liv leans in. "I'm off. Meeting Reese at his place." She heads toward the entry.

Georgia watches her leave and looks around for Vincent and Arthur. "Well, this night's turning into a dumpster fire."

"No, seriously, the band's really good!" Siaka says halfheartedly.

"Yeah, I'm really enjoying it," I say with as much enthusiasm as I can muster.

Georgia squints suspiciously. "You're both rotten liars," she says, "but if you leave me here alone, I'll make sure you're blackballed from every club in Paris." She gives us a jokey smile and turns back to the music.

"She's not joking," Siaka says.

"One hundred percent serious," I agree.

We stay where we are, trying to enjoy the music. After a few minutes, I feel Siaka's hand inching over to hold mine. He's still watching the band, but on his lips are a hint of a smile. He leans toward me, his breath hot on my ear. "We're stuck here, so we might as well enjoy it. Right?"

I twine my fingers through his and embrace the electric current as his *guérriseur* touch affects my revenant skin. I'm wondering if it can possibly feel as good to him as it does to me, when he leans over with a serious expression. I incline my head to hear, but when he says nothing, I turn.

And that's how his mouth ends up millimeters from mine. His eyes blaze, and I cross the paper-thin sliver of air between us and touch my lips to his. It's like an all-out Bastille Day celebration inside me—fireworks exploding, music pounding through my veins.

He takes my face in his hands and pulls me closer. He tastes like cherries, with a hint of mint, lips soft and warm.

The room around us disappears. The crowd is gone. It's only Siaka and me, kissing. It's the way I've wanted to kiss him since the day we met. I wrap my arms around him as he cradles my face in his hands. It feels like we're holding on to each other so we won't lose our balance and float away. He pulls back and gazes at me dizzily, before grasping my hand and turning back to face the band.

I can't breathe. I can barely stand, I'm so weak from the breakneck speed of the passion. Like I got knocked over by a powerful wave and I'm floating powerless in the surf.

"What was that?" I say next to his ear.

"We're in public, so it totally didn't count." He looks as out of breath as me but manages a mischievous smile.

"Good thing Georgia didn't turn around," I reply.

"Didn't have to." She looks over her shoulder, before turning back to the band. "Seriously, guys," she yells. "Next time, get a room."

Chapter Twenty

Vincent and Arthur return as the concert ends. The two burnouts managed to evade them, so Vincent set a watch around Liv's building in case they turned up there.

Once outside, Siaka says he needs to go home, and with a cheeky grin, gives me cheek kisses in front of everyone like nothing happened.

"Could you move those lips just a couple inches to the left?" I whisper, making his eyes pop open in surprise.

"Soon," he taunts, and takes off leaving me a tingly mess of emotions.

Arthur and Georgia leave to meet up with Charlotte and Ambrose, and I return to La Maison with Vincent, who's taking care of Odette while Kate's dormant. And for the rest of the night, I sit in front of my computer trying to work but completely unable to focus.

It's times like this that I wish Siaka didn't need to sleep. It takes all of my will power not to leave him a dozen messages, but I don't want to look like a crazy person, even if he makes me feel like one.

So, it's a huge relief when, around seven a.m., a text pops up.

Last night. Magical. Too bad about the having-to-be-colleagues thing.

I smile to myself, but a pang shoots through my heart knowing that's he's right. It's clear now. We really like each other. But we can't do a damned thing about it.

Isn't there a thing called 'colleagues with benefits'? I reply.

I'm on it…googling…and…no. 'Colleagues with benefits' does not seem to be a thing. Wait! Here's a study that says flirting at work reduces stress.

How interesting! I reply. I've been feeling pretty stressed lately.

Oddly enough, me too. Scheduling some flirting time into my work calendar. Let's say 11:00-11:15?

I sign off, and it feels like the butterflies in my stomach are making a frenzied bid for freedom.

The next few days are filled with meetings. One of the human informants who listens out for anything happening in the Paris underworld reported hearing of an upcoming gathering engineered by a powerful criminal gang based east of Paris. Now we're investigating the rumors for a link to the Numa Army.

Once again, I spend hours with Gaspard, Kate, Charlotte and Bran, when he stops by, which is most days. I sift through memories of my time with Violette, and we visit dozens of old numa haunts. We finally hit on a winning strategy when I compile a list of everyone I encountered in the numa world. Gaspard compares it to his records of numa deaths in the Final Battle and the days afterward. We discover that several numa on my list are unaccounted for, which leads to researching photos of the parties that took place in numa-owned establishments "back in the day" as Gaspard puts it. I match names with faces, and we compile profiles of numa who might be behind the Numa Army.

When I'm not with them, I'm in my bedroom working on the database. Which is a lot more fun now that every once in a while, I get a flirty note or silly gif from Siaka. Neither of us mention what happened at the concert, but the memory of the kiss replays in my mind on a constant loop.

Once in a while one of us actually slips something into our conversation. Between, How many FF do you have in Mongolia? and How can there even be fifteen revenants in Liechtenstein when the total population is something like twenty-five? there will be a, So what's your favorite film? or Have you ever been outside of France? At which point, we spin out into a twenty-minute conversation before one of us says, Better get back to the grind.

Our research on the legend of a Flame-finger who transformed humans into revenants to overthrow the Romans has turned up nothing. We've found no trace of it among the stories and "recipes" the Flame-fingers sent Bran and Siaka for the database. And Bran has found no mention of anything of the sort in his family records.

Something about the story bothers Gaspard, though, and he refuses to give up. So while Siaka sleeps at night, I fill any extra time with research in the library. Each day, Gaspard pulls out a stack of books he thinks might hold some pertinent information, and he, Bran and I scour passages about Romans and Flame-fingers for mention of a human-to-revenant formula.

Some stories are so fascinating that I forget my search and plunge in, devouring the entire book. Over the eras, bardia have repeatedly changed the course of history. Incan bardia. Egyptian bardia. Viking-era bardia. Bardia during the Atlantic slave trade. The more I read, the luckier I feel to be a part of this Machine of

Fate. I begin to understand what I could be capable of…one day. When I finally step into my role of saving humans.

Once in a while, I glance up to see Gaspard watching me. But instead of chastising me for reading for enjoyment instead of searching for clues, he returns with a wistful smile to whatever text or document he is scanning.

***

Dinner serves as an unofficial meeting time for La Maison's residents.

Odette always eats first, while we trickle into the kitchen one by one to join in on this family time. I'm even starting to enjoy it, my family-shaped hole gradually aching less, and maybe even getting smaller. Once Odette is done eating, Jeanne whisks her out into the garden for playtime so the adults can have uninterrupted conversation. Everyone shares their news over the delicious meals. And little by little the stories trickle in.

Tonight is American Night, a monthly tradition instated at Ambrose's request. The table is piled with platters of hamburgers, fries, macaroni and cheese, and coleslaw (his mom's recipe). This type of meal is beneath Jeanne's skill level, but it's clearly worth it to her to witness Ambrose's childish delight when he walks in and lays eyes on the table.

"Georgia and I have reached the third level," Arthur announces. He is in the midst of cutting into a hamburger, bun and all, using a fork and knife.

Ambrose looks on, horrified.

Spearing a piece of burger, Arthur pops it into his mouth and begins chewing.

Georgia rolls her eyes.

Ambrose shakes his head at this culinary offense. "I told you, man. I know you're medieval and all, but you just can't *do* that. You have to eat hamburgers with your hands. That's why there's bread on the top and bottom. Do you eat a sandwich with a knife and fork?"

"Yes," Arthur replies.

Ambrose facepalms. "Forget it."

Georgia pats Ambrose's hand. "I've tried, believe me."

"As I was saying," Arthur continues, "Georgia and I have made it to the third level of the Numa Army. We were invited off-Facebook to join the N.A. member site. But as soon as we entered our information, we were blocked. It's almost as if they can see past the fictional identities we created."

"Are you using the VPN I gave you?" I ask. "It reroutes you through the proxy server, so you don't appear to be connecting through La Maison's IP address."

"Yes," Georgia says. "And we use our laptops, not our phones."

I nod. "It should be fine, then. Siaka and I set up that VPN connection for maximum security."

"So, what did you have to do to get past the first two levels of the Numa Army?" Vincent asks.

"Not much," Georgia answers. "We had to engage in Facebook discussions with some of the craziest of crazypants. People who think that the US President and his cabinet eat babies. And that a deep-state conspiracy is putting mind-controlling nanobots into the drinking water. The moderators, whoever they are—and believe me, we haven't been able to get any clues on that either—let people rant on about whatever."

Arthur picks up the thread. "But we noticed that those who seem to have usable skills—like people with workout or gym selfies in their timeline, or with government or military connections—are being tagged by the moderators to join private conversations. This seems to be the way they target the type of people M wants to recruit."

"I'm posing as a physical trainer," Georgia says. "Lots of gym selfies, and motivational exercise memes. I moved right up the ranks immediately. I was tagged in a conversation and asked if I wanted to go deeper. But when I tried to sign into their page, I was refused."

"Was there an error note?" I ask.

"Just some random 'you don't have access' thing," Arthur says. "And then when we wrote the moderator to say it doesn't work, they ghosted us. We're creating new identities and trying to get back in. Just this afternoon, they began teasing a big meet-up in real life for Level Fives. Deadline to qualify is in just a few days. And I have a feeling it might be connected to the meeting the informant told us about."

You can feel the tension rise in the room. The idea of a deadline ups the ante, even if the details are sparse.

"Any luck in the library?" Kate asks.

Gaspard shakes his head. "I'm trying to deduce in which manuscript Violette might have seen the story about the Flame-finger revenant creator. I always acquire more volumes than I have time to peruse. But by now, I have read any books Violette could have seen before she died. Of course, there is always the chance that she borrowed the text from the library."

"Stole it, you mean," Ambrose clarifies, popping a fry into his mouth.

Gaspard nods, looking pained at the mere thought that something might be missing from his precious library. His life's work has been amassing every bit of revenant lore that comes available on the market, whether through rare book dealers or auction.

"How about the Judas bouncers?" Vincent asks.

Charlotte shakes her head. "I assigned three kindred from the Mouzaïa house to tail them. They've been acting totally human."

Gaspard sits back in his chair, arms crossed, and stares at the ceiling. "Let's say our theory is right, and volant numa spirits can travel from one human to another whenever they want. Surmising they have recruited dozens of level five Numa Army soldiers, primed to be possessed... How on earth are we to locate these humans before they're activated?"

"We must be vigilant and look for signs everywhere," Kate says, "not just where we expect them."

"Like that police report Henri intercepted this morning," Vincent says. "Apparently last night, a couple of guys tried to force their way past a locked entrance to the catacombs. They wanted to bring in digging equipment—one of those mini-bulldozers. When the police tried to stop them, they put up a fight, knocked out one cop with–get this! –a martial arts kick to the head. The other cop chased them by foot, but they were too fast and got away. They noticed a swastika-style tattoo on one of their arms. That detail caught Henri's attention, and he reported it back."

My phone buzzes in my pocket. I take it out and glance at the text on my screen. My heartbeat accelerates when I see who it's from then slows when I read the message.

Siaka: Can't make it tonight. Bran's tagging along with me to see my dad. But he's taking off for Brittany tomorrow, so...after that?

I type, *No problem,* then delete it, because that's not true. It *is* a problem—I'm dying to see him again. I type, *Can I come along?* then delete it, because...desperate much?

I settle for: *Can't wait.*

I hit send, then wonder if that sounds too enthusiastic. And then I think, *Well, that's exactly what I am.* Maybe it's time to be honest.

Chapter Twenty One

I spend the night trying to help Arthur and Georgia get into the N.A. member site. I even create my own false identity and attempt to fast-track myself past the virtual bouncers. But Georgia was right, the moderators seem to know that we're a threat and block and ghost us at every turn.

In the morning, Siaka's busy helping Bran pack for Brittany. The older Flame-finger wants to see his sons but doesn't want to lose precious research time. So Siaka makes sure the C2C platform works on his laptop, and packs a briefcase with Flame-finger journals, letters, and documents for Bran to go through while he is at home.

Just after lunch, Bran phones to say goodbye.

"I'll come back as soon as Kate needs me. I can do my research as well from Brittany as I can in Paris."

"You don't have to justify leaving," I reassure him. "I've been put full-time on research here in the library while everyone else is out combing the streets for clues. I guess that with the mounting danger, Kate wants to keep me tucked safely away."

"You sound frustrated," Bran says. "Don't be. Wait as long as you can to die. Kate will let you know when your help is essential."

"I know," I say. Which I do, but still wish I were with them.

Bran says goodbye and that he'll see me soon and passes the phone to Siaka.

"Is he leaving you anything to work on?" I ask.

"Nope. Feeling a bit useless. He left me a few photocopies of journals from Flame-fingers in Peru and Argentina that I need to translate before entering them into the system. But I thought I'd pick up one of his family's books tomorrow, just in case there's something there."

"Just one book?" I ask.

"We're only allowed to take books one at a time from The Archives. Security reasons."

"Ah, the famous Archives!" I say. "When are you going? I'd love to come along."

"I seriously doubt it would work. Revenants can't enter. I know you're no longer a numa and not yet a bardia, but the whole being-dead thing makes me think you'd get fried by the magical door on the way in."

I stick a marker in the book I'm researching and close the cover. "Hold on. There's a magical door that fries people?"

"It's not really a door," he says. "It looks like part of the wall in the excavations around the Cluny Museum. But when you use the right key, a signum bardia for example, or for Flame-fingers our mere presence, the wall opens into a tunnel. It's that opening that's magically protected. It's been known to get very hot when someone tries to force their way in."

"Now I really want to try it."

Siaka laughs. "Bran doesn't think there's anything of importance in the books, or we'd have already searched them. But since the Archives are down the street from my chemistry class tomorrow morning, I'll drop by afterward."

"Text me when you leave school," I say. "I'll meet you there."

"Seriously, you'll just be standing outside by yourself for a long time. It's totally not worth it."

"Watching you disappear through a magical door is totally worth it."

"If you say so," he replies, and I can hear his smile. "I have homework to do before tomorrow's class, so I better go."

"Study hard," I say and hang up.

And thoughts of Siaka and a magical door and what it would be like if I could pass through with him into the Archives, all alone just the two of us, make getting back into my research an almost impossible task.

Jeanne brings me dinner in the library, saying that the others are eating out and won't return until later. I'm getting restless from being in the same room all day, so after I eat, I take a pile of books back to my room. As I settle down on my couch for another interminable research session, my phone rings.

"Hi," Siaka says, and his voice gives me goosebumps.

"Hi back."

"So, the human half of our 'work collaboration' has to go to bed. Enjoy your sleepless night."

"Sweet dreams," I say, and hang up feeling warm and fuzzy. The word *boyfriend* pops into my mind, and I let it stay for a few delicious seconds before picking up the top book from my stack and try to concentrate.

It is a handwritten journal by a twelfth-century troubadour in Occitania who collected poems about revenants. A lot of it sounds dubious, but some stories, like the girl who died pushing a child out of the path of a team of galloping horses, and then "resurrected Christ-like three days later, only to disappear forever into the mists," sounds like a pretty accurate depiction of a bardia. I take notes for Gaspard but find nothing relating to a magical formula ensuring normal humans become revenants when they die.

Four books later, sunlight is squeezing past the curtains, spilling into a glowing patch on the hardwood floor. I put my book down and check the old-fashioned clock Jules probably bought when he was still human. It's already nine a.m. Time for breakfast. I'm thinking about the hot cup of coffee I'm going to fix myself when the words—*GET UP!*—are yelled inside my mind.

"What is it?" I ask the air.

An attack. Gaspard's volant spirit talks directly into my brain. Go down to the armory. Get suited up. There's going to be a fight. I'll tell the others.

I feel discombobulated for a second. What did he mean by, "There's going to be a fight?" Then I remember that volant revenants can see a little ways into the future, and I jump up and book it out the door. I sprint down the stairs, crashing into Arthur when I get to the ground floor. He steadies me with his hands, then jogs along the hallway beside me.

"What happened?" I ask.

"No clue," he says. "Gaspard told me to suit up."

Jeanne bursts out of the kitchen as we head down the stairs. She's carrying a tray of croissants and fruit, and bustles behind us to set it on a table. "Kate called me," she says. "She's on her way. Get some food inside you while you're suiting up. You'll need your strength."

She runs for my locker and starts laying out fight gear. "I'll help you," she says, motioning to my jeans and sweatshirt. "Take those off."

I strip to my underwear and start layering on what she hands me—a silk T-shirt overlaid by a thin Kevlar vest, black leather pants, and a long-sleeved T-shirt made of some sort of metallic fabric. Adrenaline is running through my veins as I realize I'm heading into my first real battle since I was a numa. I'm not afraid of the danger. I'm just desperate to prove myself a valuable member of my new clan.

The outside door opens and Kate and Vincent charge through, already wearing their fighting gear. "We're taking the motorcycles," Vincent says. "They'll be faster than the cars. Arthur and Louis—you take the Navigator."

Although we're in a hurry, he's giving us the SUV. It can only mean one thing—that we might need to transport a body.

"No, Gaspard," Vincent says to the air. "There's nothing more to do here. Go back to the park."

"Who is it?" Arthur asks.

"My family," Kate says.

Arthur freezes. "Who do you mean?"

Kate hesitates. "Mamie, Georgia and Odette."

Arthur's face clouds with confusion. "Georgia's supposed to be working this morning. She texted me last night to say she'd be in the office."

"She must have changed her mind," Kate says. "She and Mamie stopped by a while ago to take Odette to Luxembourg Gardens. I sent Ambrose and Charlotte with them, just in case, with Gaspard volant."

"And?" Arthur asks.

"Gaspard said that just inside the gates—in that hidden garden near the beehives—they were ambushed by humans wielding swords. Ambrose and Charlotte are down."

"Down?" I ask, not understanding.

"Dead," Kate says. "These guys mean business." The steel in her voice cracks, and Vincent takes her by the shoulders and turns her toward him.

"They want something from us," he says. "They killed Charlotte and Ambrose and haven't touched the others. They know what they're doing, or at least the numa who are controlling them do. If we give them what they want, I'm sure they'll let them go."

"Odette must be terrified," Kate says, angrily wiping away a tear. The mama tiger look in her eye would scare me to death if I weren't on her side.

"When we get there, you get Odette out of the way," she says to Vincent. Turning to me and Arthur, she says, "The two of you get Georgia and Mamie. Once you have, I'm going to hurt them."

Then she walks out the door.

I tie the steel-toed boots Jeanne has set out and buckle a belt with multiple leather sheaths around my waist. Jeanne hands me a guitar case.

"What's this?" I ask.

"Gaspard had me pack this for you last week," she says. "In case of attack. A sword, two short katanas and several daggers. He says they're your best weapons."

I nod, realizing that my workouts aren't just to build strength. Gaspard must use them to gauge my progress with different weapons. It's probably why he and Ambrose have me working with a rotating inventory of arms.

This fight is what they've been preparing me for. It's what I've been preparing *myself* for with all of the weapons practice I've done on my own for the last few years. With a stab of insecurity, I wonder if I'm ready.

"Let's go," Arthur says.

With no time to hesitate, I pick up the case packed with weapons and follow him out the door.

Chapter Twenty Two

It takes us five minutes to drive to the park, with Arthur expertly taking random side streets to avoid traffic. He swings into an illegal delivery spot, and we leap out and sprint toward the park. The only people we pass are joggers who pay no attention to the leather-clad "musicians" sprinting with instrument cases toward the park.

I spot Kate and Vincent ahead of us as we pass through the gates. We follow as they turn right and run through a narrow passageway cut through a high wall of neatly-trimmed hedges.

My heart jumps to my throat when I see what lies behind the screen of greenery. It's like a particularly gory Hollywood film. A man I don't recognize lies across the grass in a pool of blood. His head is split open like a melon. I feel sick. Like I'm going to throw up or pass out, take your pick.

And then I see, Ambrose and Charlotte. They're sprawled across the lawn, swords beside them, blood everywhere. I saw some pretty bad stuff during my time with the numa, but two people I love lying slaughtered like that is too overwhelming, even knowing that they'll come back. I lean forward for a second, close my eyes, and force the fear and horror into a space I promise myself to revisit later. When people's lives don't depend on me keeping it together. I avert my eyes from my friends, and don't look back.

Across the lawn, Kate's grandmother, sister and daughter are penned into a corner of the bushes by three men wielding swords. Georgia is screaming at one of them. "If you do so much as look in the direction of this child, I will hunt you down and castrate you in your sleep."

Next to her, Mamie holds Odette close to her, facing away from the dead bodies. Odette is putting up a fight, trying her best to escape her grandmother's clutches. "I. Want. To. See!" the little girl insists.

I only have a second to take all of this in before the two of the men catch sight of Arthur and me and run toward us. They're muscle-bound and tattooed, looking like members of a particularly violent biker gang. As they near, I see that their eyes are glazed over, and their bodies seem to be controlled by a will outside their own. Gaspard was right. Numa are possessing humans and using them like puppets.

"I'll take the one on the left. You get Erik the Red," Arthur says as I drop my case to the ground. The latches spring open, and I grab two daggers and plunge them into the sheath on my belt. Then, taking the sword in both hands, I leap up just in time to meet the man who has hurled himself in my direction.

With his wild red hair and beard, he does look Viking-esque, and though our heights are about equal, he's twice my size in bulk. He curves his sword down in a powerful swing, and I meet it with my own, blocking his blade before it can reach my face.

From Gaspard's strategy lessons, I remember that my goal is to get between him and the person I'm protecting—Kate's grandmother in this case—to defend her from that position. So, on his next swing, instead of blocking, I leap aside, let him follow through, then rush past him. His target having suddenly disappeared, he stumbles forward, loses his footing and crashes into the bushes, dropping his sword and rolling onto his side. I have the advantage, and should use it to finish him off, but I feel conflicted about killing someone who's not actually a numa. This is a man *possessed* by a numa. Is killing him still justified?

Kate is fighting side-by-side with Vincent against two of the possessed humans. They look like they're really going for it, not holding back despite their enemies' human status. But I still can't justify running over to plunge my sword into a man who's already down, so I turn my back on him and head for Mamie.

Arthur's already fighting the man closest to Georgia, and the third guy is waiting for me when I arrive. He's not even wearing a jacket, just a white T-shirt with a sleeveless leather vest, chains looping from the pockets. The broken swastika Numa Army tattoo takes up his entire right bicep, which flexes as he grips the sword between his hands.

"Get back," I yell to Mamie. She pulls Odette behind her and backs up until they're flat against the bushes.

I face the fighter. His eyes are glazed over in the same way as the Viking guy, but as I near, his gaze snaps into focus.

"I know you," he says.

I step forward, swinging my sword over my right shoulder then arcing it down as hard as I can toward his head. He lunges and blocks with a horizontal swing, bringing our faces inches from each other as our blades grind with a screech of steel. "That's strange," I say. "I've never seen you in my life."

"Not *this* life," the guy says, pushing hard on his sword and shoving me backward. I plant my heels into the ground, regain my equilibrium, and lunge forward with a slice toward his legs.

"I'm talking about before," he says, blocking my move. "You were a kid then, but I'd recognize you anywhere." He lunges, blade straight toward my chest, and I leap to the side. "You were Violette's bitch, weren't you?"

The blood drains from my face. The shame of my past rushes back with a vengeance, crashing over me like a tsunami. Inside, I'm flailing, sinking in the waves. On the outside, I stand helplessly, my strength having disappeared with those two words.

The guy takes a swing at me, and at the last second, I rouse myself and step to one side. But the tip of his blade catches my shoulder. I feel the burn of his steel slice my skin and let out a yelp of pain. Glancing down, I see red bloom on my shirt, but it's just a small patch and I can still move my arm, so the wound must be light. I lift my sword back in a defensive pose.

The man glances at my shoulder and sneers. "Still a bleeder, I see."

"What's that supposed to mean?" I ask.

"When Violette had me give you that flower tattoo…well, I've never seen someone bleed so much." He gives me a wicked smile. "A pretty tattoo for a pretty little boy. Still got it?"

Anger rises in me like a red mist, clouding my vision. I forget the reality—that this is a numa possessing a potentially innocent human—and throw myself at him. I slash fiercely with my sword, faster and more powerful than I've ever managed in practice. He's struggling to keep up, matching my blade swing for swing, blocking my moves but having no time or space to make any of his own.

I'm backing him up nearer and nearer the hedge. His attention is fully on me and not his prisoners. Mamie takes the opportunity to duck out from behind him, Odette in her arms, and makes a run for it. In a second, she's outside my peripheral vision, and I focus completely on my enemy.

I don't remember much about the numa who tattooed me, besides his sadistic grin when I cried. But that same being looks out at me now through the human's eyes, and I channel my thirteen-year-old fear and helplessness and let it drive me forward, sword held high.

I swing my blade down toward his head. But as he raises his sword to block, I quickly pull my blade backward then thrust low, aiming between his ribs, and feel my steel travel through his chest. His eyes meet mine, narrowing in pure hatred before he slumps forward and falls to the ground.

I pull my sword free and roll him over. Blade through the heart. He's dead. I feel a rush of relief—I got him before he could get me. But a heavy feeling in my chest tells me I'll have to deal later with the emotional toll of killing another human being. Breathing heavily, I turn around to assess the ongoing skirmish.

Kate is extracting her own sword from a foe who lies motionless on the ground. Vincent is still fighting, attempting to drive his opponent toward the middle of the clearing, but the other man keeps forcing him back, away from us, trying to isolate him. Kate glances his way, but Vincent shakes his head. "I'm good. Get Odette!" he yells, gesturing toward the far end of the clearing, which is hidden from my view.

"Louis, give Arthur a hand," he yells, before turning his full attention back to his foe.

I make my way to where Arthur is fighting his own battle, matching swords with the man guarding Georgia. Or *attempting* to guard Georgia.

"Stay back!" Arthur warns me, and I obey, falling back and awaiting his order. I feel helpless but know Arthur must have his reasons for fighting this man alone. He's probably afraid that something I do might result in Georgia getting injured, whereas if he's alone he's in full control.

Penned in behind the man, Georgia is pelting him with pebbles she scoops from beneath the manicured hedge. "Why can't there be any big, heavy rocks in this park?" she yells, throwing a handful of gravel at his back. He doesn't even seem to notice, which makes her even more furious. As he lunges at Arthur, she rears up and kicks him from behind with her ankle boot's stiletto heel, landing it right where his jacket hikes up from the back of his jeans.

He roars and swings backward with his sword, catching Georgia's forearm. She yelps and grabs the wound with her hand. Blood drips from between her fingers, but the way she takes her cursing up a level suggests she's not seriously hurt.

Arthur can't see that, though, since Georgia's directly behind the guy. He charges, his sword carving wide, powerful strokes. "Thou dare lay thy filthy hand upon my dearest?" he roars, switching back to the old French of his medieval days. But his anger causes him to make a fatal error. He sweeps low while his enemy's arm is up, but in his fury, he raises his head to meet the man's eyes, leaving his neck completely vulnerable. It's a move I've made in my lessons with Gaspard, when I wasn't paying enough attention. Each time it earned me a painful bruise on my neck along with Gaspard's flippant comment, "You're dead."

But this isn't Gaspard. And it isn't a practice sword. It's a numa-charged human, and the very real, very sharp sword catches Arthur on the side of his neck and slices inward. The blade lodges deep inside instead of slicing cleanly through, pulling the sword from its owner's grasp.

What takes place next happens so quickly that if I wasn't looking at just the right spot, I wouldn't know how it happened.

Georgia stands there, horrified, watching Arthur fall.

Kate yells, "Georgia, catch!" and a flashing object spins through the air between the sisters.

Georgia raises her arm and catches the short-sword in one hand. And lunging forward in a practiced move, learned in what must be hundreds of hours of fencing lessons with Gaspard, she thrusts the sword into the man's back. The blade emerges through his chest before Georgia pulls it back, letting him fall, lifeless, to the ground. Then, dropping the sword, she steps over the man and crouches next to Arthur's body. She eases the blade from his neck and cups his practically-severed head in her hands and lets out a wail of despair.

I hear a yell and turn to see that the Viking I had left sprawled in the bushes now has Mamie and Odette penned in against a hedge. He hasn't hurt them. He seems to be keeping them captive and awaiting instructions. But when he turns to see what's happening with his colleagues, Mamie rushes him, grabbing his sword arm. With one powerful sweep of his arm, he knocks her to the ground and grabs Odette.

I'm kicking myself now for not taking him out when I could, but now is not the time for regret. I have to solve the problem I made and do it quickly.

Odette is struggling and screeching, "Bad man, bad man!" while he tries to wrangle the kicking toddler. I raise my sword and start toward them but stop when I see he's pinned Odette to his chest with one hand and holds a knife to her neck with the other.

"Odette, freeze!" Kate screams. "Don't move, baby!"

And whether it's the fear in her mother's voice or the knife the giant holds to her throat, Odette does as she's ordered and doesn't move an inch.

"You! Drop your sword," the man yells at me. I open my hand and drop my weapon. I glance back and see that Vincent's fight is over. His enemy lies dead on the ground. Kate and Vincent watch the man holding Odette. They stand motionless with hands held out, either pleading with him not to do anything, or trying to calm him, I can't tell.

Georgia has stopped wailing, and sits next to Arthur, hands placed protectively on his chest. She glares at Odette's captor as if convinced she can kill him with the pure hatred shooting from her eyes.

Though I'm the closest to him, I don't dare charge him. One small gesture, and Odette could be gone.

Louis, listen! I hear the words, and for a second I think it's Kate speaking in my mind. But her eyes are fixed firmly on her daughter, her every thought on the fragile life held in the man's hands.

Don't answer back. Just nod if you hear me, the voice continues. It's Gaspard. I'm sure of it now.

I lower my chin in the slightest of gestures. Kate's grandmother is about to make a move. As soon as she does, throw your knife.

Are you kidding? I want to answer back. It's too much of a risk. If I miss, Odette could die. But I can't say anything without the Viking noticing.

Sensing my doubt, Gaspard continues. You are excellent at knife throwing. That's why I had Jeanne load your kit up with daggers. I know you can do this.

Just then, Kate's grandmother grabs a stick from beneath the hedge and swings it with all her might at the back of the Viking's legs. Before he can react, my hand is at my waist, my fingers closed around the hilt of a knife. In one fluid motion I slide it from its sheath, raise it up beside my ear, and fling it. The early morning light catches the dagger as it flies toward the giant, the slivery blade glinting brightly before embedding into his neck.

With a look of shock, the man drops both Odette and his knife. He lifts his hand to the hilt of my dagger, jerks it from his neck, and stares at it in surprise. Kate flies into action, and as her grandmother scrambles to catch Odette in her arms and pull her away, Kate's sword meets the side of the man's skull. With a clean slice, she takes off the top of his head as easily as carving a pumpkin.

The man crumples to the ground. Kate drops her sword and throws her arms around her grandmother and Odette. Then Vincent is there, wrapping his arms around the three of them, and they're talking and crying all at once.

I glance back at Georgia. She's up now, standing and watching her family, but torn between going to them and staying with Arthur's corpse.

You have to go now, comes Gaspard's voice in my mind.

"What? Where?" I ask.

I see you rushing off in a minute. You look panicked. Check your phone.

I pull my phone from my pocket and see a string of texts from Siaka.

Leaving school. Meet out front Cluny Museum in 20.

Wait…cancel. Liv wants to meet. Says it's urgent.

Hey. Back on. She said she can come here. Can you meet us at the Cluny?

And as I'm looking at the last text, a new one pops up.

Help me!

Chapter Twenty Three

In a screech of tires against asphalt, I turn Vincent's motorcycle into the street bordering the Cluny Museum. I park and check my phone. It's been seven minutes since Siaka's message and since then…silence. My heart's beating out of my chest. What could be wrong? I wonder if Liv reached him. Are they both in danger? Maybe he hurt himself somehow. No, he would have said so. I have a feeling that the danger he's in is more menacing than an accident.

I force myself to calm down and scan the area. It's nearing eleven in the morning. Normally tourists would be lining up beneath the turrets of the Musée de Cluny to visit its collection of medieval art, objects and weaponry, not to mention the museum's star exhibit, the Unicorn Tapestries. But the Cluny is closed for a whole year for renovations, "Fermé/Closed" signs plastered across its facade. Louis once mentioned that, saying the closure made it easier to visit the Flame-finger archives. Before, he'd had to sneak in late at night or early morning.

He had told me that to get there, he had to cross through the excavation site in the below-ground area that contained the ruins of Roman baths. At street level, a barrier runs along the perimeter of the site, but I home in on a spot in the chain link fence where a door is hung with an "employees only" sign. Sure enough, the padlock is missing and the door slightly ajar. Glancing around to make sure no one's watching, I slip through and ease it closed behind me before heading down the metal stairs.

The excavation is a huge open-air pit dug in a wide area around the museum itself. The skeleton of stone walls that once housed the Roman baths form a two-story tall maze through the space. I head past them to the edge of the excavation—a sheer wall of dirt and rock rising straight up twenty feet to street level.

It's dark along the wall, the sunlight unable to reach the bottom of the pit, so it takes a few minutes for my eyes to adjust. No one is here. I walk a bit further, turn a corner, and there they are. Siaka, Liv and a guy I don't recognize grouped around an opening in the earthen wall.

The magical door leading to the super-secret Flame-finger archives is wide open. The fact that a stranger is standing with Siaka in front of it makes my blood run cold. This is bad. Very bad.

As I approach, I see that the guy is tall with shoulder-length blonde hair and wears jeans and a camouflage jacket. He blocks the door with his body, with Siaka and Liv facing him. His grin widens when he catches sight of me, causing the others turn to see what he's looking at.

Siaka looks terrified. "I shouldn't have texted you. You should leave!" He sees the blood on my shirt and freezes. "You're hurt!"

"It's barely a scratch." I ignore his warning and walk steadily forward, drawing my sword as I near.

"So that's why you've been stalling," the guy says to Siaka before turning his attention back to me. "Oh well. The more the merrier."

I cast a glance at Liv. She wears her regular impenetrable look—pissed off, but not scared. *What's going on?* I think. I continue toward them, gripping my sword before me in both hands.

"You can stop right there," the guy says when I'm a stone's throw away, "and drop the weapon." Something about his evil smile looks familiar. I ignore his command and dig back in my mind to five years ago…and I recognize him. I just made a profile for him a few days ago. One of the numa who was unaccounted for after the Final Battle. "Maurice."

"Louis," he replies. "Violette's toy. I would say how nice it was to see you again, but I'd be lying. I thought you'd be off fighting those soldiers I sent to distract you and the rest of your kindred."

My expression gives away my surprise. He laughs. "Don't tell me you've managed to beat them already! How disappointing. It looks as though humans are too feeble to be trusted with missions of any importance."

Liv laughs, as if she doesn't include herself in the species he just insulted. And then it dawns on me. Liv came with Maurice. She brought him, knowing Siaka was coming to the archives. But why?

The information sinks in on a level deeper. This must be the "Reese" Liv's seeing. She's dating a numa. Liv, who created our communications platform. Who has access to our database. Which means…Maurice has probably seen everything. Why in the world would she do that?

My eyes meet Siaka's. "Are you okay?"

He shakes his head, no, and his eyes flick back to Maurice. It's only then that I see that Maurice has his own sword, as he nudges back one side of his duster to show its hilt.

"Like I said, drop the sword," he says.

"Or what?"

"Or I'll kill your boyfriend."

Liv throws him a look, and he nods at her. Collusion. Satisfied, she turns back to me, and crosses her arms. *She has no idea what this guy is*, I think. *And no idea he would kill her cousin without batting an eye.*

"Maybe you can talk Siaka into finally giving me what is mine," she says.

"What would that be?" I ask.

"The *guérriseur* gift. If my mother had taken it, like she should have, I would be the Flame-finger."

I keep my sword pointed at Maurice but shift my gaze to Siaka.

"I can't give it to her," he says with despair.

"You can," Liv says bitterly. "But you won't."

"Why are you doing thi—?" Siaka begins.

"She's doing it because I need something." Maurice cuts him off. "You see, there's a particular *guérriseur spell*, or whatever you would call it, that I've been searching for ever since Violette mentioned it to me. It doesn't seem to be among the data entered into the C2C."

Like I suspected, Liv gave him access to our databases. Alarm bells ring in my mind. How much does he know?

"I was hoping we would find it in the Flame-finger archives," he continues. He shifts his gaze to me. "I've already tried to access them from the other side of the wall. I recruited some volunteers from my Numa Army to dig through the catacombs to get there.

Didn't work. Now Siaka here refuses to fetch the notebooks for me, and we revenants are barred from going in through the door."

At this, he pokes the empty space in the wall. There is a crackling sound, and sparks fly from his fingertip.

"Ow!" He shakes his hand and laughs. "See? Protected by *guérriseur* juju. And Liv can't go in because she's not a Flame-finger."

"Yet," she corrects him, looking hatefully at Siaka.

"But you don't even want the gift!" I say. "You told me you wouldn't like working with the bardia, saving people's lives."

"I don't plan on being Flame-finger for the *bardia*," she says, and takes Maurice's hand. "I'm going to work with Reece."

When she told Siaka about Maurice, she had conveniently left out the part about his being a powerful numa. One who, I remembered, was close to Lucien, Violette's predecessor as head of the numa. Like Lucien, Maurice had been convicted of horrific war crimes during World War II, one of those historical figures whose transformation into a numa was no surprise. I wonder how much Liv knew of *that* story. Or if she even understood what the numa were.

"Let me guess," I say to Maurice. "You're after a way to turn humans into revenants. You're trying to build an army."

"Bingo!" he says. He draws his sword and moves toward Siaka. I realize he's been blocking the tunnel entrance so Siaka wouldn't dash inside for safety.

"Okay, fine." I lay my sword on the ground, hold my hands up, and take another step forward so that we're standing in a triangle. Maurice and Liv are in one corner: Siaka and I at the other two angles.

Maurice glances approvingly at my sword. "Now we can handle this like reasonable adults. Siaka, give Liv your power…or I'll kill you both."

"What?" Liv says, glancing up at him doubtfully, but Maurice doesn't look at her.

"No," Siaka says.

"Fine." Maurice shoves his sword back into its hilt. Then, with a lightning-speed gesture he whips out a knife and holds it to Liv's throat.

"Whoa, now!" I say, raising my hand to stop him.

"What the hell!" Liv says, struggling.

"Trust me," Maurice murmurs.

If Siaka looked afraid before, now he looks downright stricken. "Okay, fine. You know how this works," he says to his cousin. "Did you bring a paper and pen?"

She nods and jabs an elbow into Maurice, who lowers the knife. She drops her bag to the ground, pulls out a notepad and pen, and hands it to Siaka. He takes it from her. With a trembling hand he writes something down. Then, ripping the page off, he hands them back, trying to catch his cousin's eye.

She avoids looking at him, stuffing the items back into her bag before standing and shoving a cigarette lighter toward him. "Burn it," she says. "You know that's how it works."

"Liv," he says, pleading.

"Only one of us gets the gift," she replies. "There's no reason it shouldn't be me."

"I don't care about the gift as much as I care about your safety," Siaka says. "You can't help these people. They're…"

He stops as Maurice takes a step closer to Liv, still brandishing the knife. Siaka's shoulders slump. He hands the paper to Liv, and she reads it out loud. It's in another language, so I can't tell what she's saying, but it sounds like a single phrase. Once she's done, he brings the lighter close and sets the paper on fire. Liv holds up the note, making sure the fire catches. Once it does, she lets go and allows the burning paper to float toward the ground.

Something happens.

A kind of magical glow leaves Siaka and begins inhabiting Liv.

"Yes!" she crows, waiting until the process is completed. Then she sprints toward the open door in the wall. She raises her hand and reaches gingerly toward the darkened entryway. Her fingers pass the place where Maurice received a shock.

Nothing happens. No sparks. No frying skin. She can pass safely through the invisible barrier.

"It worked!" she calls triumphantly. She pulls her phone out of her pocket, turns on the flashlight and disappears into the tunnel's gloom.

Maurice turns to me, a wicked smile on his face. "So tell me. How are things at La Maison?"

Chapter Twenty Four

For a tense fifteen minutes or so, the three of us stand there. An occasional gust of wind blows from the tunnel, smelling of mildew and wet clay.

Siaka and I steal a look at each other, and Maurice taps the hilt of his sword, reminding us what will happen if either of us makes a move. Siaka looks devastated, as though someone has just died. Which, I'm sure it must feel like—his cousin just stole the birthright his dead mother gave him.

Finally, there's a sound of footsteps from the tunnel, and Liv appears in the opening, holding her bag up victoriously. "Look, Reece! I have them," she says to Maurice. "All five books."

"That's my girl," he says, lips twisted in a cruel smile.

She steps through the magical doorway as nonchalantly as if she were exiting a subway. "Let's go!" she says impatiently, pointedly avoiding looking at me and Siaka.

"We're not quite done yet." Maurice's words are like lava, hot and glowing with malice.

"What do you mean?" Liv replies. "We have the books and the gift."

"Yes, but the gift won't work for my purposes until you're transformed," he replies.

Her brow furrows. "Transformed into what?"

"You want to be the numa Flame-finger? You have to be a numa first."

Liv looks confused. "And?"

"You might not be clear about the fine print," Maurice says. "To become a numa, you must betray someone to their death. You took the first step by bringing your cousin here and stealing his gift. Now all that's left is the part where he dies. Would you like to do the honor, or should I?"

"Wait a minute," Liv says, with a haunted expression. "I agreed to the betrayal part, though it should have been my gift in the first place. Whatever. But you swore you wouldn't hurt Siaka."

"Technically speaking, it will be so fast, it won't hurt him. Not much, at least." Maurice lifts the knife and aims it at Siaka's head.

"No!" Liv and I yell as one. But while she freezes, my reaction is immediate.

Lunging down, I scoop up my sword and swing it hard, knocking the knife from his hand. It lands with a thud on the ground a few feet away.

"You are starting to annoy me," he growls, drawing his sword and thrusting it my way. I squeeze the hilt tightly to keep his powerful stroke from knocking my blade to the ground.

"Run!" I yell and brandish my weapon toward Maurice. In my peripheral vision, I see Siaka charge toward Liv. He attempts to pull her away.

"Stop it!" Liv yells, twisting to break free.

Siaka shoves her behind him, shielding her with his body. "You idiot! He plans on killing you right after he kills me!"

"Her death will only be temporary," Maurice replies calmly. He spins sideways and deals me another heavy blow. I skip backwards and his sword strikes the ground with enough force to send up a spray of dirt and pebbles.

"You don't know she'll turn into a numa." I back away, readying myself for another round. "Gaspard says it's impossible to detect if someone's predisposed to become a revenant."

"Well, he doesn't have access to the same source materials Violette did," Maurice says. He charges toward me, initiating another violent round of sparring. I'm just able to keep the pace.

Maurice pulls back and pauses. Sweat gleams on his brow. He looks me up and down, like he's searching for a chink in my non-existent armor.

"What exactly did Violette tell you?" I ask.

His lips form a twisted smile. "She said that if a Flame-finger dies betraying someone to their death, they become a numa. Automatically. Finding one to join her was in Violette's plans. Bran's mother refused her and... Well, you know the outcome. But while Violette didn't live long enough to find another willing Flame-finger, I did." Then, moving so quickly I don't have time to react, he shifts his sword to his left hand, draws a dagger from beneath his coat, and throws it.

"No!" I yell. I lunge to protect Siaka, but it's too late.

The blade flies and lodges so deeply into his chest that only the hilt is visible. His mouth opens, his eyes grow wide, and he lets out a groan.

Liv shoves Siaka forward. "Get out of my way!"

Siaka keels over, falling in slow-motion. He lands on his knees, propping himself up with one hand and pressing the other to his chest, as if checking to see if the knife is actually there.

"What's wrong with you?" Liv says. But she freezes when she spots blood pooling on the ground beneath him. And then she sees the knife. "What the fuck!" she screams at Maurice. Throwing herself down next to Siaka, she scrambles to help him lie down.

The ensuing second of silence is split by an anguished cry. It's only when I'm running toward Maurice, sword raised, that I realize the cry is coming from me. I swing my weapon furiously. I don't even think about what moves to take, my anger propels me forward. Maurice's sneer disappears, and now he's really fighting.

It's as intense as the three-way sparring with Ambrose and Gaspard, but with only one foe. And maybe because this thought is in my mind, when a voice appears, I recognize it as Gaspard's disembodied spirit and don't miss a move.

Hold him off. I've told the others what's happening. They're on their way.

The news that my kindred will be arriving acts like kindling to my flame, and I'm gaining on Maurice when something whizzes by me and strikes him on the forehead. I back up, keeping my blade lifted, as we both turn to see where the missile came from.

Siaka is lying on his back, eyes closed, pressing Liv's wadded-up T-shirt to the wound. She stands a few feet in front of him, stripped down to her tank top. Her face is red with fury. In one hand she clutches a couple of stones and in the other she holds the bloody knife. She chucks another rock at Maurice, missing this time, and screams, "What the hell! You probably killed him, you psychopath!"

Maurice's sneer returns. "That was actually the point," he says. Then, turning his attention back to me, his eyes widen in shock as

I thrust my dagger deep into his side. He looks down at it and roars.

Releasing the hilt, I sprint toward Siaka. Throwing myself down, I kneel over him. "Are you okay?" I gasp.

His face is pale. His shirt is sopping with blood. "I'll be fine," he says through clenched teeth. His eyes are glazed with tears.

"You don't look okay." I carefully lift the bunched-up cloth he's holding to his chest. The wound is deep, and from the amount of blood pumping out of it, I'm guessing his heart was pierced.

He shakes his head as if it doesn't matter. "Don't let him kill Liv. Get her through…" He stops and squeezes his eyes shut, before forcing them open again. He searches my face.

"What? Get her through what?"

And then I understand.

I hear a roar from behind me and turn to see Maurice marching furiously toward us like that robot cop in Terminator. The red stain on his shirt is proof I wounded him, but it obviously wasn't bad enough to stop him.

I scramble to my feet. Aiming carefully, I fling my dagger toward Maurice.

With his attention on Liv, Maurice doesn't see it coming. It lodges deep into his bicep, but he doesn't even flinch. Yanking it out with his left hand, he hurls it back in my direction. It whizzes past me, and I exhale in relief. Then I realize he wasn't aiming for me. I turn and see the knife planted in Siaka's neck. His eyes are wide and unblinking.

Liv stares aghast, heedless to the fact that Maurice is heading toward her with sword drawn. I pick myself up and run straight for her, desperately trying to reach her before Maurice. And when

I do, I ram her like a linebacker, plowing her toward the doorway in the rock. As we reach it, I give her a shove, and she stumbles through, falling to the ground inside the tunnel entrance.

For me, touching the invisible force field is like hitting an electrified fence. A sharp current courses through me as the magical entrance repels me. I pitch backward, landing on my back on the ground.

And that is how I'm lying when Maurice steps up into my line of vision, sword raised above his head, point aimed at my chest. With a roar, he plunges the blade downward, driving its tip through my heart. My chest explodes with pain, and my body convulses with the shock. My vision floods with black, like ink spilling over glass. And then I am gone.

Chapter Twenty Five

I dream I am walking on water. My feet skim across its surface, step after step. When I reach the middle, my feet sink down and touch the silt. The water is ice cold, numbing my skin.

On the other side of the stream, I see people waiting for me. They are surrounded by blazing auras, the flames licking and crackling in haloes around their heads.

I force myself to look back from where I came. Another group of people stand on the streambed behind me. Their auras are different—suspended in the air like red mist.

Violette stands at the front, her birdlike form leaning forward as if she wants to charge into the water and drag me back. Behind her are numa who I recognize from my past. Maurice sneers at me, baring his teeth.

I turn back toward the far bank and wade in the direction of the people with the burning haloes, sloshing through rivulets that cascade over my numb feet toward some distant destination downstream.

The faces of the assembly become clearer. I recognize Ambrose first. He's twice as big as everyone else. Next to him is Charlotte, and next to them—standing so close together that you couldn't slip a piece of paper between them—are Gaspard and Jean-Baptiste.

I thought he was dead. I dismiss the thought as quickly as it comes. This place exists outside life and death, I understand. This is the eternal: past, present, and future.

Jules and Ava are on the other side of Charlotte and Ambrose. They smile at me, then turn toward each other and exchange a tender glance.

I see Charles and Uta and Arthur and a whole host of other people I don't recognize. As I approach, Vincent and Kate step forward. They hold their hands out to help me up. Kate's halo flares like a supernova; I squint to look her in the face. As I hold my hands out to them, I notice that Vincent isn't wearing his usual suspicious expression. Instead, his smile is genuine.

"Welcome, *kindred*," he says.

They pull me from the water, but I don't move. It's as if my feet are stuck in cement. The others group around them and reach toward me, a host of hands to drag me from the stream. The water sucks me back, reluctant.

"Jump toward us, Louis," Kate says, her eyes flashing like sapphires in sunlight. "You have to give it everything."

I push against the stream bed with all my might. The others give a mighty pull. I feel a sharp pain, as though joints are being pulled from sockets.

Then, something gives way.

Chapter Twenty Six

I bolt up, gasping for breath.

My chest feels flat. My eyes struggle to open, feeling like sandpaper. Fighting waves of panic, I struggle to figure out where I am. Then I recognize the antique enameled lamp hanging from the ceiling above me, and I realize I'm in Jules's room.

My room.

La Maison.

Glancing around, I realize that I am lying on my bed, dressed in a soft, clean pair of sweatpants, T-shirt and hoodie. No more blood-stained fighting gear.

Someone saw me naked, I think. Then I realize how stupid it is to be embarrassed. This must happen all the time in La Maison. Everyone will have seen everyone else naked. Wounded…dead.

I fill my lungs, which sends me into a coughing fit. The door flies open, and a halo of inky hair appears. It's Gaspard. At least it's not Ambrose or Charlotte or someone else who would make a scene.

He turns into the hallway, "He's awake!"

Bran pushes past him, rushing toward me.

Gaspard follows and, picks up my hand, pressing a finger to my wrist. "Good pulse. Slow, but strong."

"How are you feeling?" Bran inspects my face.

"I'm," I croak, and launch into another coughing fit.

Gaspard hands me a glass of water from a tray sitting next to the bed. I drink it down in one.

That's when it dawns on me.

It happened.

I'm a bardia.

Because I died saving…

My death scene flashes before my eyes.

Siaka bleeding out on the ground. Me shoving Liv to safety inside the mouth of the cave. Maurice looming over me with a look of pure, unadulterated fury as he plunged his sword into my chest.

I pull up my shirt and see the smooth skin on my chest. My body healed itself while I was dormant. I'm alive. But Siaka…

Suddenly I'm scrambling out of bed, but Bran and Gaspard block my way.

"Don't get up yet," Gaspard says. "You'll be too weak to walk for several hours."

"Where's Siaka?" I demand. That's the first thing I can think about.

Immediately, Bran turns his gaze away.

Gaspard can barely look me in the face. "I'm sorry. He didn't make it."

It feels as though Maurice is thrusting his sword into my chest all over again. The searing pain is no less. Siaka. Dead. I fought Maurice. I gave it my all. But I couldn't save Siaka.

"Have another drink of water." Gaspard refills my glass and presses it to my lips. "Fig?" he asks. He plucks one from a fruit bowl and pops it into my mouth. I chew twice before realizing that I'm ravenous and, pulling the bowl from the bedside table onto my lap, start devouring walnuts and grapes and cherries.

Gaspard looks encouraged. "Without sustenance you won't regain your strength."

"Tell me," I say between mouthfuls. "Please. What happened?"

Gaspard shoots a glance at Bran who nods his approval. "You were fighting Maurice. I visited you, volant, and told you, I had alerted Kate and Vincent of what was happening."

I nod to show that I remember. "Wait, Odette. Is she okay?" I ask, the scene from the park flooding back to me.

"Amazingly, she is fine," Gaspard said. "I'm sure you'll see her soon. She keeps asking about you and trying to come in to see you."

I feel comforted, and Gaspard continues. "Kate and Vincent arrived on the scene minutes after you were killed," he explains. "Maurice had been attempting to coax Siaka's cousin to come out of the cave, but when he saw Kate and Vincent, he fled. Vincent took chase but lost him. When Kate confirmed that both you and Siaka were dead, the cousin…Livia?" Bran nods at him, and he continues. "She became hysterical. Kate convinced her to accompany us in the ambulance that transported your bodies back to La Maison."

Bran takes over the story. "As soon as Kate phoned, I came right back from Brittany, but Liv left before I could arrive and speak with her. Apparently, she told Kate that she blamed herself for everything. She said she had to leave France or Maurice would hunt her down. Kate offered to send her to stay with Charles in Berlin, but Liv said she'd rather rely on her own network of contacts. We have no idea where she is now. Her mother is frantic."

"And Siaka's father?" I ask.

"My cousin is in mourning." From Bran's tone, it's clear that he shares the same grief for his lost nephew.

I reach out my hand to him and let the tears course down my cheeks. Bran and I sit there crying for a moment, and then I say, "Liv forced Siaka to give her the Flame-finger gift so that she could retrieve the revenant-creation formula for Maurice from the archives."

Bran nods sadly. "She gave Kate a full confession, including that Maurice had recruited her to be the Flame-finger for the numa."

"Not just a Flame-finger for the numa," I say, trying to contain my anger. "A *numa* Flame-finger. He had promised her eternal life but didn't specify that she'd have to die after betraying her cousin to his death."

"What?" Gaspard looks like he's been slapped. Clearly, Liv had skipped this part when confessing to Kate.

"Maurice was trying to coax Liv out of the cave because she had already betrayed Siaka, so all that was left was killing her and taking her back to his lair or whatever. That way, she would animate three days later a fully-fledged numa Flame-finger, capable of helping him build a Numa Army from regular humans using a technique he hoped was in the books."

"Why in the world would Maurice think Liv would animate?" Gaspard asks. "The chances of that happening are one in—"

I interrupt him. "That's the thing. Maurice was carrying out Violette's plan, conceived before she died. She had found an ancient text that said that any Flame-finger who betrayed a human to their death would automatically become a numa."

Gaspard is the first to speak. "Hold on. Numa and bardia share the same DNA. It's only their actions in life that predict what they will become in death. So, if a Flame-finger automatically becomes a numa after betraying someone to their death, it is possible that they would also become a bardia if they die saving someone."

My mind is grasping at the possibility, hope inflating like a balloon in my chest, but then I remember something, and the balloon pops. "I don't think the rule applies to any *guérriseur*. They have to be a Flame-finger. Maurice didn't have Liv steal Siaka's gift simply to raid the archives. It was so that she was sure to become a numa upon death."

Gaspard and Bran look at me blankly. I try again. "Siaka gave Liv his gift. He wasn't a Flame-finger anymore when he died."

Bran gets a burning look in his eyes. "Once a Flame-finger, always a Flame-finger."

"Where's Siaka now?" I ask, my voice trembling.

"His coffin is downstairs," Gaspard says. "We scheduled the funeral for tomorrow, so that you would be able to say goodbye." He clears his throat. "The others said you had a special bond."

I launch myself up so forcefully that I manage to push past Bran and Gaspard. I get halfway across the room before collapsing in a heap. "Help me up!"

"You need sustenance," Gaspard says, grabbing a bottle of water and making me drink.

Bran helps me stand, and we stagger together toward the door.

"Stand aside, my friend," Gaspard says, and scooping me into his arms begins carrying me down the stairs. For a second I can't believe this thin, middle-aged man is carrying me, and then I remember how strong he is when he fights, and that when it comes to revenants, you can never judge by appearances.

Once in the front hall, Bran opens the door for us, and there, in the middle of the sitting room, an open coffin sits on a table. Inside, Siaka is tucked into a nest of green satin padding, his arms folded across his chest and his face drained of color. Someone's dressed him in a white button-down shirt and a navy suit jacket, which makes him look even less like himself than the whole drained-of-life thing. Tied around his neck, hiding the place where Maurice's dagger entered Siaka's neck and killed him, is a beautiful blue silk scarf.

My heart feels ripped out of my chest. Siaka is dead. It's the first time I've felt this strongly about someone. And knowing he was murdered by such a vile leach of a man, after being betrayed by his own family, well it's too much. I take a step toward him, and my knees buckle. Gaspard wraps a firm arm around me and walks me to the side of the casket, helping me stand. Reaching in, I brush my fingers against Siaka's cold cheek, then tentatively begin to work the knot on the scarf.

"Are you sure this is such a good idea?" I hear Jeanne say from behind us, but Bran hushes her. The knot finally loosens and I slowly unwrap it, afraid of what I'll see. Preparing myself for the torn flesh where the lifeblood poured from...my boyfriend.

The silk scarf falls to one side, and my heart stops in my chest. Siaka's skin is perfect and smooth. The wound is gone.

"It's healed!" I cry, and Gaspard and Bran jump into action.

Jeanne takes Gaspard's place, propping me up so that I can watch. "Ssh," she coos, brushing my hair out of my face.

Propping Siaka's head up, Gaspard forces his lips open, pouring a small amount of water into his mouth. The water spills out the sides of Siaka's mouth and his head lolls back. Bran holds Siaka's hand between his and rubs frantically, trying to get the blood flowing again.

"Siaka," Bran says. "Can you hear me?"

Gaspard gives the water another try, but it puddles on either side of Siaka's head drenching the casket pillow.

"Maybe he'd respond better to someone else," Jeanne says softly. She helps me turn so I can lean over the casket, propping me up so my legs don't give out. I smooth Siaka's dark curls with my fingers, then lean over and give his forehead a gentle kiss.

With all of the emotion in my heart, I say, "Siaka, wake up."

My heart beats once. Twice. A muscle twitches in Siaka's forehead. Then, furrowing his brow and squinting, his beautiful green eyes open and look into mine.

Chapter Twenty Seven

"Louis, what's taking you so long?" A voice calls from outside my door. It's Charlotte.

"Come in!"

She steps in. Her blonde hair is loosely attached with a sprig of white lilacs and tumbles down her bare shoulders over a shimmering copper floor-length dress.

"Wow, you look gorgeous."

"And you look like a mess," she says, laughing.

"I don't know why I chose a real bow tie." I yank the purple silk from beneath my starched collar. "I should have gotten a clip-on. I can't figure this thing out."

"Clip-ons are for losers." Charlotte grasps the two ends of silk, flips and twists them, pulls tight, then turns me toward the mirror. She tucks my shoulder-length hair behind my ears. "There. You look handsome. But, if we don't leave right now, we're going to be late."

I grab my jacket, shrug it on, and give myself one last glance in the mirror. It's the first time I've ever worn a suit. Although it feels as though I've dressed as a grown-up for Halloween, I can't help but be pleased with the effect.

Ambrose is waiting for us in the jeep, drumming his hands on the steering wheel along to jazz music blasting out of the windows. Catching sight of us, he hops out and jogs around to open the passenger door for Charlotte, helping her sit without wrinkling her dress. "You get more beautiful every single day," he murmurs, closing the door carefully behind her.

Seeing me watching, he loses the lover-boy look and tries to look dignified. "That comment was *not* meant for you," he says, "though I gotta say, thanks to the last month of workouts, you're almost filling out that suit jacket." He gives me a friendly punch on the shoulder. I make a mental note to check the spot later for a bruise.

Ten minutes later, we're pulling up in front of La Sainte Chapelle, the tiny church at the middle of Ile de la Cité, barely a stone's throw from Notre Dame Cathedral. Ambrose tosses the key to a parking valet wearing a white rose on his collar.

Got to hand it to Georgia, I think. For her event-planning business to arrange valet parking in the center of Paris, she must have some great connections.

Ambrose whisks Charlotte out the passenger side and places her hand atop his arm. "Shall we?" he asks.

She leans up to give him a peck on the cheek.

"I don't get a real kiss?"

She shakes her head. "Nope. Lipstick."

Ambrose laughs his ground-rattling baritone laugh and takes his wife in his arms, quite likely squeezing the life out of her and probably wrinkling the dress at the same time.

"Don't mind me. Third wheel," I murmur, following them through the security checkpoint. We walk into a courtyard festooned with flowers and ribbons and join a short line of stragglers who are as late as us.

I know everyone from sight, if not by name. A couple of bardia from the Mouzaïa house as well as some from further abroad. I hear a British accent and a couple speaking German. La Sainte Chapelle is a small space, so these guests must have been hand-picked. As I understand it, a larger reception is planned later today.

"Come in, come in! It's about to start," says a middle-aged man with an American accent and a sprig of white lilacs fastened to his lapel. He ushers us through the darkened lower chapel toward the winding steps leading upstairs.

"Theo, my man!" crows Ambrose, giving the man a back-clapping hug. "All the way from New York City. Share a plane with Jules and Ava?"

"Yes, for the first and last time," the man chuckles. "The cuteness. It was suffocating." He smiles and reaches out to shake my hand. "I'm Theodore Gold. You must be my new kindred, Louis."

"Brand new," I confirm. "Practically a baby compared to you."

"Time flies so fast. It seems like it was only yesterday when I was human," he says, following me up the stairs. "Gaspard told me about your renewed problems with the numa. I hear Ava will be staying to help Kate locate the remaining numa outside of Paris."

"Everyone's hoping the two of them will be able to find the numa nest and flush them out," I say.

"You don't sound so sure."

"I was one of them. I doubt they'll just sit pretty and wait for two Champions to pick them off." This is the new me talking. I'm not proud of who I was, but I have learned to use it in the service of my kindred.

"Yes, well, I will be staying for a little while in case there's anything I can do to help," Theo says as we arrive at the top of the stairs. At which point we fall silent because the scene before us is breathtaking.

I've visited La Sainte Chapelle before. Years ago, on a school trip. So I know what to expect. But still, I feel overwhelmed when I step into the long single room, forty feet high, with colorful stained-glass windows stretching from floor to roof. There's barely any wall to be found. Just one narrow, towering stained glass window after the other, divided into sections that tell every story in the Bible in order.

It's like being inside a kaleidoscope. Jewel panes with sunlight coming through, casting prisms of color everywhere. A string quartet sits at the far end of the chapel, beneath a canopy of white roses, playing a classical piece. On either side of them are full-grown lilac trees that must have been dug up and transplanted into giant pots just for this occasion. Lilacs…Kate's favorite. Even from the back of the room, I can smell the fragrance.

Between the string quartet and me, there are probably one hundred people seated on folding chairs brought in for the occasion. We're clearly the last to arrive; almost all the seats are taken. Jules and Ava wave to us from the front row, indicating they've saved two spaces for Ambrose and Charlotte.

Charlotte whispers to Ambrose, "This is *so* exciting!" and they make their way down the central aisle, stopping every few paces to greet people.

I look out over the crowd, searching, but not finding. Then a voice comes from behind me.

"Hey, handsome. Fashionably late?"

I turn, and my breath catches in my throat. Siaka is wearing a grey suit over a black shirt accompanied by a silk tie and pocket square the color of ripe apricots. But I barely catch that—all I can see is his face. His brown skin, glowing with health. Jade green eyes sparkling with amusement. Only a month ago, he was a corpse, and now?

Well, now…

I take his face in my hands and pull him into a kiss.

It's a kiss that says, I'm so happy to be here with you. Not to mention, You're so hot that even though we're in a room full of people, I can't keep my hands off you.

Siaka leans back and smiles. "You know we're in a church, right?"

"Yeah, but I haven't seen you in over twenty-four hours," I respond. "That's more than a day without a kiss, which has got to be some sort of sin. So, this is the perfect place to do penance."

"You are insane," Siaka says, laughing. He pulls me back in for another kiss. Then, he takes me by the hand. "Seriously. We better hurry. Bran's saving our seats."

He leads me towards the second row, where two chairs sit empty next to Bran and Charles. As we take our seats, Ava and Jules turn to greet us. In a stage whisper she says, "Louis. So good to see you again. And you must be Siaka. We've heard so much about you."

"The American Champion. It's an honor," he says, leaning forward to give her the *bises*. I've forgotten how stunning she is. I know a part of it is the same magnetic Champion allure that Kate has, but it's clear that Ava was remarkable even before she animated. It's practically impossible to take your eyes off of her.

Jules reaches over to shake Siaka's hand. "I'm Jules, no honorific title. Nothing special about me…not now that she's around."

Siaka laughs. "Nothing special? That's not what I've heard. Your exploits are legendary, man."

Ava eye rolls and holds up a hand. "Don't even start," she says, and then leans in toward Jules for a playful kiss. "He's mine now. His past stays firmly in the past."

Jules's expression shows how smitten he is. Siaka sits back, grabs my hand and holds it between his. The look he gives me makes it feel as though all this adoration is contagious.

Which it clearly is.

"If this wedding doesn't start soon, it's going to become a full-on orgy of love," Uta says from beside Ava. Then raising an eyebrow, she leans in to kiss Faust.

Bran seems set on ignoring the PDA happening around him, which makes me grin. How he managed to romance his ex into having two children with him, I can't even guess. As Gaspard strides to take his place at the front of the chapel, I hear Bran murmur, "Just in time."

The string quartet lowers their instruments, and the congregation falls silent. Everyone cranes their heads toward the back of the room. After a beat, the music starts back up—a joyful melody—and three figures make their way up the aisle. In the center is Kate's grandmother, Mamie, wearing what looks like a Chanel suit in pink tweed with matching heels so high they could trip a supermodel. She walks with chin held high, as if striding through a room full of undead superheroes is not only her right but *their* privilege.

On either side are Vincent and Arthur. They wear matching dark suits with brightly-patterned bow ties. Arthur is breaking tradition, wearing modern garb to his own wedding instead of medieval. His shoulder-length blond hair is tied back in a loose ponytail. And Vincent? Well, Vincent looks like a Greek god, his thick black hair flowing back in long, shiny waves.

They look happy enough to burst right out of their suits. As they near our aisle, Vincent looks over, sees Siaka next to me, and gives me a cheeky wink. Over the last month, he's made up for not accepting me initially by doing everything he can to show me I'm a valued member of the kindred.

As they approach the first set of pews, they let Mamie take her seat, then proceed to stand on either side of Gaspard. He can barely acknowledge them; his gaze fixed on the back of the chapel.

Siaka leans in and whispers. "I can't believe that both the head of France's bardia and probably the oldest guy in the room are both nervous as…" He searched for the right term.

"As grooms on their wedding day?" I suggest.

"Exactly!"

Siaka's right. Vincent is fiddling with his cufflinks, and Arthur is fidgeting with his collar. You'd never guess both of them had died dozens, maybe hundreds of times in horrific circumstances, bravely offering themselves up to pain and mutilation.

But I forget all about them when the quartet starts the Wedding March. All of us rise out of our seats and turn.

Murmurs of delight ripple through the crowd as Odette strides seriously down the aisle wearing a dress that Jeanne has been working on for the last month. "Hand-smocking," she called it, the bunched top scattered with embroidered pink and white rosebuds. Odette tosses white and pink petals from a basket, and when she joins Mamie at the front, she asks in a whisper loud enough for all to hear, "How did I do?"

"Very well, my cabbage," Mamie reassures her, pulling her granddaughter in to stand next to her. Then, looking back, she puts her hand to her mouth and her eyes well with tears.

I turn to see what she's witnessed.

The entire congregation breathes in all at once. I can't breathe. I reach blindly for Siaka's hand, find it, and squeeze the hell out of it so I won't burst out crying. I'm not normally a crier. But watching those three figures walk down the aisle, arm-in-arm, almost melts me into a puddle of tears.

In the center of the group is Kate's grandfather, Papy, with noble nose and full head of cotton-white hair. I've met him a couple of times in the last month. He's stopped by with Mamie to see Odette and pulled me aside to express his gratefulness for my part in saving his great-granddaughter. The crooks of his arms accommodate the hands of his granddaughters. The three of them pace in time to the music.

Georgia's strawberry blond pixie cut is grown out long enough to curl up at the sides. Her hair is topped with a wreath of white poppies. Her light-gold dress is straight out of The Great Gatsby. Floor-length. Satin. Sleeveless. Dipping at the neck and draping low in the back. A train in the same fabric spreads out behind her.

Kate wears the same dress, but in a light silvery color. Her long brown hair is curled in waves and crowned with a wreath of brightly-colored flowers. She looks like a goddess of springtime or nature or beauty. Maybe all three.

They all beam as they stride down the aisle.

Siaka leans over and whispers, "Find a man who looks at you like Vincent looks at Kate."

I tear my eyes from the brides to look at the grooms, and see that Vincent is transformed. I've often seen him gaze at Kate with an expression of awe and surprise, as if he can't believe he's lucky enough to be with her. But this look beats them all. Maybe it's because she's making The Statement in front of everyone.

She chooses him.

I shift my gaze to Arthur. As he watches Georgia walk toward him, he looks as though he's about to burst out in tears. I have to look away so I won't do the same.

"This is my first wedding," I whisper to Siaka. "Are they all this emotional?"

"Nah," he says as the brides pass us. "This one's on steroids."

"Maybe it's because Kate turned Vincent down so many times," I venture. "She told me it took Odette and her grandmother almost dying for her to change her mind and ask him."

"And it took Arthur actually dying in front of her for Georgia to ask him," Siaka adds.

Arriving at the front, the brides each lean in to give Papy a kiss on the cheek, then leave him with Mamie and go to stand with their grooms. The looks passing between the two couples are electric. You can practically hear it crackling and see the sparks fly.

"I can't even," Siaka says. He glances down at our entwined fingers and squeezes my hand tight in his. "I refuse to cry at a wedding."

"Just don't look up," I tease him. "I'll give you a running commentary. Okay, the grooms are basically devouring the brides with their eyes. And…vice versa."

"Ssh!" Bran jabs me with his elbow.

Gaspard tells everyone to have a seat. "Welcome bardia of France, England, the United States, Germany, Spain and places further flung. I also welcome all who are not here… Our friends waiting at La Maison, unable to attend due to the crowd limit allowed by Paris's rigorous fire safety standards."

Everyone chuckles and Gaspard gives one of his bashful smiles.

"I won't talk for long. Both couples have written their own vows…" Georgia interrupts him by raising a finger. "Correction," Gaspard adds. "Georgia's vows were written by an American poet named…" He glances down at his cue card. "Johnny Cash."

Georgia looks pleased and nods for him to go ahead.

"You all know how important symbols are to us. For example, the symbol that proves a human has been taken into our confidence and can be trusted."

At this, Papy and Mamie stand and hold up the *signum bardia* pendants that Gaspard gave them a few years ago. Georgia and Kate touch their *signum bardia* necklaces. Georgia's are made of pearls and Kate's of sapphire. On either side of me, Bran and Siaka stand. They pull back their sleeves and hold up their arms to show their own tattoos.

"Welcome kindred," a hundred voices say as one, and the acoustics of the hall make the words echo before fading. Kate's grandparents, Bran and Siaka take their seats, and Siaka grabs my hand between his again. I grin and nudge his knee with mine.

Gaspard resumes. "The *signum bardia* signals *our* chosen ones. Whereas the vows these couples trade today signal to us *their* chosen ones. A symbol of a choice."

"A choice they took their sweet time making," Ambrose murmurs.

"So, before I make a mess by saying something way too old-fashioned, I will allow these four beloved kindred to take over and officiate their own wedding. Love will guide their words."

Gaspard steps aside and Kate and Vincent begin their vows.

"Who knew Gaspard was so romantic?" I whisper.

"I *know*," agrees Siaka, placing his hand on his chest. "'Signaling to us their chosen ones?' Heart melting."

We sit silently, listening to the couples' vows, but I'm too distracted to take anything in. There's something I want to say to Siaka. Now, not later. But I don't dare mess it up by whispering. What if he doesn't hear? Or understand?

Wait till later, I urge myself. But, unable to resist, I take Siaka's hand, flipping it over to place it upright atop my knee, using his palm as a writing pad. With my finger, I trace out the letters:

S I A K A…

I…

C H O O S E…

Before I can finish, he pulls his hand from mine and traces on my palm with his own finger: *Y O U.*

His eyes meet mine and we both smile. It's a smile that agrees we're together. It's a smile that admits we've only just begun. It's a smile that says we've all the time in the world. All the time to know each other.

Lifetimes, actually.

Acknowledgements

Jumping back into the revenants' world has been a wild ride. But after hundreds of messages from you, my readers, I decided to take on the mission. The result? Louis and Siaka and a reunion of the beloved members of La Maison.

Thanks to those friends who provided a sounding board…

Reading manuscripts to each other with Laura Lam, the two of us poolside atop a volcanic cliff in Ischia, Italy. (Our one big trip between lockdowns!) Brainstorming with Mags Harnett in Paris and Dublin. Read-throughs by Lori Stephens and Claudia Depkin. Conversations about story with Celeste Rhoads.

To my soul sisters—Kim, Diana and Mags—for providing unconditional love always, no matter what shit comes down.

Much gratitude to Hannah Kaner, her dad Ben, and the entire Kaner family for allowing me to escape Paris to their Normandy house over two years during Covid. The dead blackbird falling down the chimney next to the fire mere feet away from where I was musing (and, ugh, eating) was an omen that magic will always reign over La Fericotière.

I finished the book while perched upstairs in Conor Horgon's beautiful house in central Dublin. Thank you.

To Tara Weikum for helping me shape DIE FOR ME into what it is today.

Huge thanks to Karen Ball at Speckled Pen for the edits (and for deleting my dozens of "just"s). Also to Jas Poole for the gorgeous cover!

Most of all, to my two favorite people, Lucia and Max. You bring more joy and laughter to my life than I thought possible. I can't believe I gave birth to the coolest people I know. (As well as the most patient.) As I read you the drafts, you listened, laughed, and swooned. Plus, you always asked the golden question: what happens next?

And again, to my readers. Years after the Revenant Series began, you are still sending me notes. I am humbled at what happened when my story met your minds. You allowed me to bring something remarkable into this world. For that, I will always be grateful.

About Amy Plum

Amy Plum is the international bestselling author of young adult novels, including the DIE FOR ME, AFTER THE END, and DREAMFALL series. Her books have been translated into thirteen languages. Amy grew up in Birmingham, Alabama before venturing further afield to Chicago, Paris, London and New York. An art historian by training, she can be found on most days either daydreaming or writing (or both) in a Paris café.

Read on for a look at Amy Plum's

Die Once More

Die Once More

This one-hundred-page novella picks up where the international bestselling Die for Me trilogy ended and follows the eternally irresistible Jules Marchenoir as he leaves Paris behind for a fresh start in New York City.

Jules is a revenant—an undead being whose fate forces him to sacrifice himself over and over again to save human lives. He's spent the last century flirting his way through Paris and, most recently, falling in love with his best friend's girlfriend. Loyalty and heartbreak have led him to choose a new life in NYC.

Separated from his friends and his home, Jules is adrift in this dangerous new world, facing unknown enemies . . . until he meets a revenant named Ava. Though the battle for France has been won, an epic war between good and evil has just begun in the Big Apple, and Ava needs Jules's help to uncover the key to an American victory. Jules finds himself in the same position he crossed an ocean to escape: at risk of losing his immortal existence as well as his heart.

Chapter One

A new city. A new land. A new life. Or so I had hoped.

I left my friends, my country, the home I've had for a hundred years to escape a girl who has seen only seventeen summers. I put an ocean's distance between us just to discover it wasn't far enough.

We traded places: She's now in Paris, and I'm in New York. And therein is the problem. This is Kate's town, and it's like she never left. She's still here. She is everywhere.

In a week of walking the city streets, I feel like I've seen her a hundred times. From the American accents of high school girls chatting loudly on the subway to the downtown teenagers wearing her uniform of T-shirt, slim jeans, and Converses. She is in all of them, peering out of their eyes, taunting me with a love I will never taste. Because her heart is with another—my best friend, Vincent. I love him like a brother, but right now couldn't be gladder about the four thousand miles of ocean between us.

I wrap my coat tighter around me and lean out over my rooftop vantage point. Below me, chunks of floating ice turn the East River into one of the frozen martinis that seem to be endlessly flowing at my New York kindred's parties. For a bitingly cold daybreak the first week of March, the Paris sky would be spread with a blanket of gray clouds. But here in Brooklyn, where the sun has just risen, the sky is a dazzling field of cornflowers. The diamonds it casts on the surface of the water blind me. Bring me to tears. Or at least, provide a good excuse for my stinging eyes.

I hear a whistle, and turn to see my kindred Faust waiting for me next to a door shaft sticking up like a lone tombstone in the middle of the football-field-size roof. I make my way toward him, passing the barbecue pits and the giant swimming pool: all covered and hibernating. Waiting for the ice to melt and the city to move the party back outside again. The endless party. Life's a party in New York.

What am I doing here? I ask myself for the hundredth time. Surviving, is the correct response. The only way I know how.

"Council's ready for you," Faust says, clapping me across the shoulder as he guides me down the stairs.

"So I don't get it," he says. "You and your kindred come to New York a week ago on a mission to re-embody your kindred Vincent. You succeed, he goes back with the others, but you decide to hang out here at Frank and Myra's house. Then Vincent calls you to Paris, and after barely twenty-four hours in France you're back in New York?"

"What can I say? They were up against Violette and her army," I say, avoiding his point.

Faust nods. "Yeah, I guess you can't turn down a request from your kindred to help out with Paris's final battle against the numa. Man, what I would have given to be there and watch the Champion kick numa ass."

"It was a spur-of-the-moment thing," I respond. "Only room for twelve on Gold's plane. I would have brought more of you if I had understood what was going down."

"Frank and Myra . . . they're still in Paris, right?" Faust asks, eyes sparkling with good-natured jealousy. "I can't understand why you came back last night and didn't stick around for the after-party," he says, and then, seeing my blank expression, shuts up.

After a few seconds, he murmurs, "Man, we could sure use your Champion here. We've got our own bad stuff going down. But I'm sure you've heard all about that."

I follow him down six long flights of stairs. This building is massive, taking up a whole city block. Faust explains the floor plan as we descend.

"So you've already seen the roof. Next floor down, the seventh floor, is exhibition space, concert hall, and—as you probably saw last night—party headquarters. It's the only floor allowed to humans. That's why it has a dedicated elevator and stairway that don't access the other levels."

Faust points to a wall where industrial-size elevator cars are caged in by retracting metal gates. "Those go down to the basement. Man, you have to see that. It's so huge, there are actually two antique railroad tracks down there—used to bring goods in and out. At the front of the building we have river access for boats, and a dozen ambulances. The armory's down there too. Basically everything that's high security, and the stuff we don't want people to see, is belowground."

We exit the stairwell on the ground floor and begin making our way down the cavernous stone-gray corridors toward the front of the building. As we walk, I try to get a reading on Faust. He's got this regimented air, but not as much as a soldier or policeman. And he struts straight-backed, but with his arms slightly spread, like his muscles are getting in the way. He's already built big but has doubled his size with some serious time in the gym. Like most guys I've seen here, he favors facial hair: long razor stubble for him. Taking a wild guess, I would peg him as a fireman. I wonder if that's what he was before he died.

"So I've given you the layout. Now let me explain what it's all about," Faust says, switching into tour guide mode. "The building's a New York landmark, built of reinforced concrete in 1913 for a food processing company and then abandoned in the fifties."

I nod, and he continues. "Gold scooped it up for a song and made it our secret headquarters. No one realized we were operating out of here until the nineties . . . at which point it was decided to make it an open secret."

We turn a corner, and I begin to hear voices echoing through the cavernous corridors. "To the community, we're a bunch of artists, musicians, and young independent businesspeople— creative types—who've been granted these luxury living and working spaces by an arts foundation. We 'give back to the community' by opening the place up for exhibitions, concerts, and the monthly intel-gathering 'block parties' like we had last night."

He smiles at the memory of the epic party on the top floor of the building that just ended a few hours ago. It was in full swing when I arrived from the airport. I passed through, grabbed a drink, and spent the rest of the evening alone on the roof, until, after dawn, I saw the fleet of revenant-driven taxis shuttle the last partygoers home.

No partying for me. Not last night. Not with the gore of battle still fresh in my mind. Not after witnessing the permanent death of Jean-Baptiste, our leader. And in the midst of it all, my lovely Kate, fierce and beautiful and no longer human. I needed time to process it. To remember. To heal.

"It's the best spy network ever," Faust explains, jerking me back into the here and now. "The locals offer us up valuable information on our enemies without even knowing what they're giving us. The council always meets immediately after to discuss what we learned. So—perfect timing for your official welcome." Faust and I turn a corner and are in an airy, sunlit space occupying the entire front section of the building, overlooking the waterfront. A kitchen that could easily provide for several restaurants is fitted along the wall at the back. And between it and the floor-to-ceiling windows is a café area with around fifty tables. These are artfully grouped around potted trees strung with Christmas lights.

"This is where I leave you," Faust says, gesturing toward a gathering of ten tables arranged in a large circle. Several dozen of my New York kindred are seated there, waiting for me in a solemn silence. I move to stand behind the one empty chair left at the "head" of the circle—the one with the prime view of the river.

A familiar figure, dressed all in white, stands at the far end of the table to greet me. "Bardia of the five boroughs of New York, I present to you Jules Marchenoir, longtime Paris kindred," says Theodore Gold. "Witness for yourselves: His aura confirms him as one of us. Having met him before, I personally vouch for his goodwill, and I know that he is highly esteemed by the kindred of his birthplace."

"And I personally vouch for this man's ability to seduce half the human population of London without even breaking a sweat," interrupts a muscle-bound guy who could be Ambrose's older brother, drawing laughs from around the table. He holds up a fist, which I bump with my own as I take my seat next to him. "Met you at the '97 London convocation. Coleman Bailey, Harlem Riots of '43," he says, repeating a tradition I'd noticed with American revenants: introducing themselves with a detail of their death.

Gold chuckles, taking his seat, and says, "Sorry for the formal tone, Jules. There's a formula for introducing out-of-town revenants to kindred. Besides having a high number of immigrants, Americans also tend to move around a lot."

I nod and accept a glass and pitcher of water from the man sitting on my left. "We're used to formalities in the Old World," I say, trying my best to sound light. This is the last place I want to be: in the hot seat, having to explain myself to a lot of strangers while my brain is melting and my heart is in tiny jagged pieces—in a language that is not my own. But it's a necessary evil. If I want to stay, they need to know why.

My face has given something away: I see compassion on my kindred's faces. One girl speaks up. "We were so sorry to hear about Jean-Baptiste," she says, and everyone else nods and adds their own words of condolence.

Gold speaks up. "We're going to make this brief, Jules. No formal inquisition necessary. In America we don't have leaders, or 'heads,' like you do in Europe. Everything is done democratically. I usually speak for the crowd, since I am the official American historian—somewhat like Gaspard is for you. But any New York revenant animated over twenty years can be on the council, and it holds all the power."

Gold pauses and looks around the group, waiting to see if anyone wants to jump in. When no one does, he says, "You have expressed a desire to join us here in New York. Could you give us an indication of how long you plan on staying?"

Here we go. "An indeterminate amount of time, if you are willing to host me," I respond.

I see curiosity burn behind the eyes of the bardia. A member of the council speaks up. "Can you tell us the purpose of your stay?"

"I need time away from Paris," I say.

"Wouldn't your kindred prefer you to stay closer . . . say, elsewhere in France?" she presses.

"At the moment, I was hoping for a bit more . . . distance." This is harder than I thought. If I could say it in French, I could add the innuendos needed to imply that it was a personal issue and they could mind their own damn business. But their expressions show openness and willingness to help me, so I swallow my bitterness. Note to self: They're not the ones I'm upset with.

"Your kindred called you back to France to fight with them barely two days ago," someone says, "and you complied. But you returned to New York last night—immediately after the battle. Can we conclude that this break from France is your decision, and not something wished for by your leaders?"

I take a moment to formulate my response. "My kindred would prefer that I stay. It is my decision to leave. But I am here with their blessing."

"We will not be perceived as taking your side in any type of personal dispute, then, if we welcome you among us?"

"Definitely not," I respond.

Everyone seems to relax. So this is what they were digging for.

Another man speaks up. "Thank you for the clarification. Jean-Baptiste named Vincent the head of France's revenants the same day you defected. We were worried about becoming involved in a power struggle."

I shake my head. "Vincent is the best man for that job. I support him fully." They are awaiting further explanation, but I'm not going to give them any. I'm not about to announce that I'm here because I'm heartbroken. That the woman I love is in love with my best friend. That it will kill me if I have to see them together any longer.

Around the table significant looks are being thrown among council members, and there is a general nodding of heads. A man with a mustache and a strong Southern accent speaks up. I have to listen closely to understand him. "Frederick Mackenzie, American Civil War. I'm acting administrator of the Warehouse. So far, you've been staying in the Greenpoint house. Gold says he put you there temporarily, since you knew Frank and Myra from a convocation. But we ask all newcomers to the New York clan— whether you're freshly animated or an old-timer from out of town—to live here in headquarters for the first six months. That way you can learn our ways without being an unwitting security risk just because you did things differently back home. After the six months, you are welcome to join a house in the borough of your choice, or, like many of our more sociable kindred, decide to stay here."

He pauses, and I nod to show I understand.

"Pre-council kindred often serve as welcome reps. Faustino, who you have already met, has been assigned to you. He'll be happy to show you around, explain the rules, and fix you up with your basic needs. Is there anything else we can do to make your transition to America easier?"

I'm not sure what to say. They're so . . . efficient.

A woman sitting next to Gold jumps in. "For those of you who don't already know of him, Jules Marchenoir is an accomplished artist. Perhaps those involved in the visual arts could provide him with necessary supplies, get him set up with a studio, and tell him when the life drawing group meets."

The woman is stunning—in an exotic kind of way: long black hair, copper-colored skin, almond eyes, and high cheekbones. I rack my brain but am sure I haven't seen her before. I would have remembered. So how does she know me?

"Thank you," I acknowledge gratefully.

She nods, but frowns, like the interaction is distasteful to her. Like I've offended her.

How bizarre. I must have met her before—it had to have been at a convocation. Did I try to pick her up or something? I doubt it—I restrict true flirting to human girls for just this reason. Why risk offending someone who could hold a grudge for eternity? Not to mention the danger of them falling in love. And who wants that?

Or at least that's how I used to think. Pre-Kate. She changed my game. Now I'd give up all the flirtations in the world just to be with her. Something pings sorely in my chest, and without thinking, I raise my hand to press it, drawing concerned looks. My kindred think I'm mourning. Let them. I am.

Gold breaks the silence. "Anyone else have a question?" He peers around the table. "No? Well, then I'll speak for all of us to say, 'Welcome, kindred.' We're glad you're here, Jules Marchenoir."

"Welcome!" several say together, like a cheer. People rise to go, several crowding around me to introduce themselves. Several ask about the French Champion—Kate. They want to know more details about how she emerged, and it is quickly obvious that their own numa problem is beginning to approach what we experienced in France.

My gaze drifts across the table to the girl who spoke earlier. A group of people stand around her, and the face that was stony with me is now radiant as she speaks with them.

A beautiful girl. Normally that would draw me like a moth to flame. Even with my no-kindred-lovers rule, a bit of playful banter and a shower of compliments (and the enjoyment of her inevitable response) would do my spirits a world of good. But not now. I don't even have it in me to say hello.

Her eyes lift and meet mine, and the coldness is like an ice ray.

What? I ask her silently, shrugging my confusion.

She rolls her eyes—actually rolls her eyes!—and turns her attention back to the person she's talking to.

Disconcerted, I look back to a man standing with his hand out and remember that I'm supposed to shake. No bises—cheek kisses—of course.

Faust appears and stands by my side as the room empties. "Need anything?" he whispers to me.

"Yes," I whisper back. "I would give my immortal soul to get out of here and walk."

Printed in Great Britain
by Amazon

50243156R10121